HONORÉ
DE BALZAC
A PASSION IN THE
DESERT

ALAN SUTTON
1985

Alan Sutton Publishing Limited
30 Brunswick Road
Gloucester

Copyright © in this edition 1985
Alan Sutton Publishing Limited

British Library Cataloguing in Publication Data

Balzac, Honore de
  A passion in the desert.
  I. Title
  843'.7   PQ2159

  ISBN 0-86299-249-4

Cover picture: detail from Pyramids of Gizeh *by*
Thomas Seddon
The Fine Art Society, London

Typesetting and origination by
Alan Sutton Publishing Limited.
Photoset Bembo 9/10
Printed in Great Britain
by The Guernsey Press Company Limited,
Guernsey, Channel Islands.

CONTENTS

BIOGRAPHICAL NOTE

At the time of his death in 1850, Balzac had written almost a hundred novels and stories, as well as plays and pamphlets, while maintaining an extensive correspondence and regular journalistic output. Yet this author, who has been called 'the Shakespeare of the novel', had a less than auspicious childhood and early life and showed little or no promise of the genius that was later to develop in Balzac the man.

Honoré de Balzac was born on 16 May 1799, in Tours, France, into a family of modest means. His father, whose real name was Balssa, was of southern peasant origin and had no claim to the aristocratic 'de' which he, and later his son, Honoré, assumed. Bernard Francois de Balzac, or Balssa, had risen to the middle class, moved to Paris and there married a Parisian girl over thirty years his junior. From 1798 to 1814, the family lived in Tours and it was there that Honoré de Balzac was born and lived as a child. His schooldays were undistinguished and he appeared slow and even stupid as a pupil. His childhood was coloured by his mother's temperament, which was of a neurotic and fluctuating nature. Although Mme de Balzac outlived her son, she never understood him and continued to treat him as a child until his death. The only real friend of his youth was his sister, Laure, who was also to be his first biographer.

In 1814, on the downfall of Napoleon, the family returned to Paris, where Balzac studied for a further two years before becoming a lawyer's clerk until 1819, when his parents agreed to giving him a meagre allowance that would permit him to devote his time to literary pursuits. Balzac's first efforts at writing were unremarkable to say the least. Between 1820 and 1825 he lived with his parents, his attempts at living in a garret having failed. Much of the work produced in these early years was positively bad. After 1825 Balzac lived alone again and in that time pursued a great number of grandiose, mad and generally impractical schemes, whose purpose was to make money. These schemes included becoming a publisher, buying a printing house and a typefoundry, while continuing to write. This mania for speculation was to pursue Balzac throughout his life and by the age of twenty-nine he was saddled with debts of around 100,000 francs which, despite efforts and sacrifices made by his family and many women friends, he was unable to repay before his death. On the verge of bankruptcy in 1828, Balzac took up his pen seriously and in 1829 *Les Chouans*, his first work of any note, was published. This work was written in the Romantic manner of Walter Scott and its subject was the royalist guerillas who fought in western France in 1799. Also published in the same year was *La Physiologie du mariage*, an anonymous, satirical work whose subject was cuckoldry. Balzac sought to demonstrate both the cause and the cure for this social problem and in so doing betrayed a powerful and sympathetic understanding of women that was to be the basis for many of his greatest works of fiction.

Between 1828 and 1834, Balzac lived in central Paris leading a tumultous existence, spending freely and often vulgarly; frequently, the fat dandy aroused hilarity by his sartorial indulgences. But despite his eccentricities, Balzac was fairly well received by Paris society, not least because he was a brilliant raconteur. Avid of fame and fortune, not to mention love, Balzac never lost sight of his own potential. He wanted to be recognised not only by the 'dry' world of letters, but also by the fashionable, artistic circles that gave Paris its colour and charm. However, social ostentation was then, as later, merely a form of relaxation from incredible stints of writing. Balzac frequently worked for fourteen to sixteen hours at a time, often through the night, wearing a quasi-monastic gown and subsisting on vast quantities of black coffee. If his method of working was extreme, his method of printing was even more so. He exasperated his printers by sending them skeletal drafts to print and then writing over and over the type with a maze of erasures, insertions and emendations. This manner of arriving at the finished copy was, of course, prohibitively expensive and Balzac usually found that he had spent the fee for writing a work on printers' bills, before the book was even published. Balzac's tremendous creative urge was balanced by an equal urge to make money and the paradox between his desire and his ability was a subject frequently explored in the novels.

From his early twenties, Balzac formed liasons with a number of women. The plebian Balzac usually set his sights on 'grande dames', with results that were not always happy. His earliest serious relationship was with Mme de Berny, a member of the old French aristocracy, who was already twice Balzac's age when they met in 1822. Until her death in 1836, Mme de Berny assisted Balzac both morally and financially. She divined his genius at an early stage and nurtured and encouraged the young man with an understanding and tolerance that he had never known before, nor would again. She was the model for several of Balzac's characters of mature and feminine women and in the year of her death he dedicated to her the soft and gentle prose of *Le Lys dans la vallee*. After the publication in 1831 of *La Peau de Chagrin* (The Wild Ass's Skin), Balzac received a letter (in 1832) that was to alter the course of his life. The letter was from a Polish noblewoman, Evelina Hanska, who was married to an aged and wealthy Russian landowner. Like many other women, Mme Hanska wrote to express her admiration for Balzac's work. They met twice in Switzerland in 1833; the second time they became lovers and agreed to marry on the death of Count Hanska. Balzac's letters to Evelina Hanska were published posthumously as *Letters à l'étrangère* (Letters to a foreigner) in four volumes, between 1889 and 1950. (Mme Hanska's own letters are not extant.) The correspondence gives a fascinating and invaluable insight into both the life and work of Balzac. In spite of his growing devotion to Evelina Hanska, Balzac began a relationship with Sarah Frances Lowell in 1834. She was the English wife of an eccentric Italian count and to Balzac, Sarah, who was to be his friend, patron and mistress for many years, was 'la contessa'. In 1835, Balzac had a brief affair with yet another Englishwoman, Lady Jane Ellenborough. The number of Balzac's lady friends is seemingly endless and they caused Mme Hanska, in her Ukranian home, many transports of jealousy.

In 1835 Balzac moved from central Paris to the suburb of

Chaillot, partly to evade creditors and writ servers. During 1833–4 Balzac conceived the idea of grouping his novels into a composite whole which would include novels already published, such as *Eugenie Grandet*, and those still to be written. The idea of the theme 'provincial life' matured during 1834, a landmark in Balzac's life. The plan was to have three main categories of work: 'Etudes Analytiques' (Analytic Studies), dealing with the principles of human life and society; 'Etudes Philosophique' (Philosophical Studies), revealing the causes determining human action and 'Etudes de Moeurs' (Studies of Manners), showing the effects of those causes. These three 'study groups' were further sub-divided into six 'scènes', of private, provincial, Parisian, political, military and country life. It was not until 1840 that Balzac chose the Dantesque title *La Comedie humaine* for the entire body of work, which by 1848 totalled seventeen volumes. As early as 1845, Balzac had already begun to plan a 'definitive' *Comedie humaine* with a consortium of publishers. This was published posthumously between 1869 and 1876.

Balzac's retreat to Chaillot stemmed chiefly from his unabated attempts to make money and between 1836 and 1842 the abortive ventures continued apace. Highlights of Balzac's schemes included unsuccessful attempts to edit *La Chronique de Paris* (1836) and *La Revue Parisienne* (1840); an expedition to Sardinia on a mining quest; and the construction of a fantastic house near Versailles in 1838 which was abandoned in 1840 for a house in Passy, which is now the Balzac museum. Success in the theatre and election to the Académie Francaise also eluded him at this time.

Apart from his writing, his socialising and his ventures, Balzac also maintained an insatiable interest in occult theories and 'weird' practices. He was an addict of unusual learning and read widely and quickly into topics as diverse as geology, mesmerism, Swedenborg's theosophy and architecture. However, in 1842 an event occurred that was to indirectly hasten Balzac's untimely death, but also to increase still further his output of work. In that year, Balzac learnt of the death of Wenceslas Hanska and felt that he now had good expectations of marrying Evelina. In fact she held back for many years; his debts were an obstacle, as was her coldness and past jealousies.

Balzac persisted in his ambition of marrying her and much of his self-destructive and often superhuman effort was aimed at reasserting his stature in her eyes, as well as improving his financial position. They met in 1843 and from that date their life was a series of meetings and holidays together. A pregnancy and a tragic miscarriage followed, and loneliness and misgivings prevailed between them; Balzac especially was lonely as his health declined rapidly. Between 1847 and 1850 Balzac spent most of his time at Mme Hanska's chateau of Wierzchownia; but not until March 1850, when Balzac was desperately ill, did Evelina relent and agree to marry him. They returned together to Paris, too late to enjoy their marriage or Hanska's wealth, for Balzac died only a few months after the wedding, a burnt out and exhausted man.

Balzac is generally regarded as the father of realism, or naturalism, in French literature. His own nature was certainly a paradox – a man of incredible energy and vision, with a superabundant imagination which was harnessed in a most fruitful way to remarkable powers of realistic observation. Despite, or perhaps because of, Balzac's own bourgeois background, he was able to create a world peopled with over 2,000 characters as 'alive' and believable as any walking, breathing people. Balzac's own life was often more extravagant, more incredible and certainly more ostentatious than most of the characters in his novels. Balzac is not among the great French stylists of the nineteenth century, his work does not have the flow or rhythm so admired by critics of the twentieth century; he hammers home his point of view until it becomes, in the words of Gautier, 'le style necessaire, fatal et mathematique de son idee'. One of the major criticisms levelled against Balzac, is that his works are too narrow, too sordid and too purely bourgeois in subject. His work has also been accused of bad taste and sentimentality, not to mention hypocrisy (he deplored the opportunist *nouveau riche* in whom he lived out his most ambitious fantasies through his work). Balzac's work reflects his life more accurately than almost any other writer. He *was* sentimental by nature, he almost certainly *did* have bad taste, but he was also far too clever a man not to recognise the paradoxes in himself, just as he perceived them with such painful clarity in others. Human nature does not change as rapidly or as fundamentally as economic or social conditions and the bad taste and sentimentality that Balzac lived and wrote about is as powerfully present, as true and as pointed in this last quarter of the twentieth century as it ever was. Balzac's ambition was to 'compete with the civil register', to picture his contemporaries in all their ways. In this he succeeded, but many would argue that he went even further and showed the power of human nature over human effort. The chief question to be asked is, how deep did Balzac's understanding really go? Most of his readers would agree that he plumbed the depths.

ZÖE SCHRAM-EVANS

A PASSION IN THE DESERT

A PASSION IN THE DESERT

'It is a terrible sight!' she exclaimed as we left the menagerie of Monsieur Martin.

She had just been witnessing this daring showman 'performing' in the cage of his hyena.

'By what means,' she went on, 'can he have so tamed these animals as to be secure of their affection?'

'What seems to you a problem,' I responded, interrupting her, 'is in reality a fact of nature.'

'Oh!' she exclaimed, with an incredulous smile.

'You think, then, that animals are devoid of passions?' I asked her. 'You must know that we can teach them all the qualities of civilised existence.'

She looked at me with an astonished air.

'But,' I went on, 'when I first saw Monsieur Martin, I confess that, like yourself, I uttered an exclamation of surprise. I happened to be standing by the side of an old soldier, whose right leg had been amputated, and who had come in with me. I was struck by his appearance. His was one of those intrepid heads, stamped with the seal of war, upon whose brows are written the battles of Napoleon. About this soldier was a certain air of frankness and of gaiety which always gains my favour. He was doubtless one of those old troopers whom nothing can surprise; who find food for laughter in the dying spasms of a comrade, who gaily bury and despoil him, who challenge bullets with indifference – though their arguments are short enough – and who would hobnob with the devil. After keenly looking at the showman as he was coming from the cage, my neighbour pursed his lips with that significant expression of contempt which superior men assume to show their difference from the dupes. At my exclamation of surprise at Monsieur Martin's courage he smiled, and nodding with a knowing air, remarked, "I understand all that."'

'"How?" I answered. "If you can explain this mystery to me you will oblige me greatly."'

'In a few moments we had struck up an acquaintance, and went to dine at the first restaurant at hand. At dessert a bottle of champagne completely cleared the memory of this strange old soldier. He told his story, and I saw he was right when he exclaimed, "I understand all that."'

When we got home, she teased me so, and yet so prettily, that I consented to write out for her the soldier's reminiscences.

The next day she received this episode, from an epic that might be called 'The French in Egypt'.

During the expedition undertaken in Upper Egypt by General Desaix, a Provençal soldier, who had fallen into the hands of the Maugrabins, was taken by these Arabs into the desert beyond the cataracts of the Nile. In order to put between them and the French army a distance to assure their safety, the Maugrabins made a forced march, and did not halt till night. They then camped by the side of a well, surrounded by a clump of palm trees, where they had before buried some provisions. Never dreaming that their prisoner would think of flight, they merely bound his hands, and all of them, after eating a few dates, and giving barley to their horses, went to sleep. When the bold Provençal saw his enemies incapable of watching him, he picked up a scimitar with his teeth, and then, with the blade fixed between his knees, cut the cords that lashed his wrists, and found himself at liberty. He at once seized a carbine and a dagger; provided himself with some dry dates and a small bag of barley, powder and balls; girded on the scimitar, sprang on a horse, and pressed forward in the direction where he fancied the French army must be found. Impatient to regain the bivouac, he so urged the weary horse that the poor beast fell dead, its sides torn with the spurs, leaving the Frenchman alone in the midst of the desert.

After wandering for some time amidst the sand with the desperate courage of an escaping convict, the soldier was forced to stop. Night was closing in. Despite the beauty of the Eastern night he had not strength sufficient to go on. Fortunately he had reached a height on the top of which were palm trees, whose leaves, for some time visible far off, had awakened in his heart a hope of safety. He was so weary that he lay down on a granite stone, oddly shaped like a camp-bed, and went to sleep without taking the precaution to protect himself in his slumber. He had sacrificed his life, and his last thought was a regret for having left the Maugrabins, whose wandering life began to please him, now that he was far from them and from all hope of succour.

He was awakened by the sun, whose pitiless rays falling vertically upon the granite made it intolerably hot. For the Provençal had been so careless as to cast himself upon the ground in the direction opposite to that on which the green majestic palm-tops threw their shadow. He looked at these solitary trees and shuddered! They reminded him of the graceful shafts surmounted by long foils that distinguish the Saracenic columns of the Cathedral of Arles. He counted the few palms; and then looked about him. A terrible despair seized upon his soul. He saw a boundless ocean. The melancholy sands spread round him, glittering like a blade of steel in a bright light, as far as eye could see. He knew not whether he was gazing on an ocean or a chain of lakes as lustrous as a mirror. A fiery mist shimmered, in little ripples, above the tremulous landscape. The sky possessed an Oriental blaze, the brilliancy which brings despair, seeing that it leaves the imagination nothing to desire. Heaven and earth alike were all aflame. The silence was terrible in its wild and awful majesty. Infinity, immensity, oppressed the soul on all sides; not a cloud was in the sky, not a breath was in the air, not a movement on the bosom of the sand, which undulated into tiny waves. Far away, the horizon was marked off, as on a summer day at sea, by a line of light as bright and narrow as a sabre's edge.

The Provençal clasped his arms about a palm tree as it if had been the body of a friend; then, sheltered by the straight and meagre shadow, he sat down weeping on the granite, and looking with deep dread upon the lonely scene spread out before his eyes. He cried aloud as if to tempt the solitude. His voice, lost in the hollows of the height, gave forth far off a feeble sound that woke no echo; the echo was within his heart!

The Provençal was twenty-two years old. He loaded his carbine.

'Time enough for that!' he muttered to himself, placing the weapon of deliverance on the ground.

Looking by turns at the melancholy waste of sand and at the blue expanse of sky, the soldier dreamed of France. With delight he fancied that he smelt the Paris gutters, and recalled the towns through which he had passed, the faces of his comrades, and the slightest incidents of his life. Then his Southern imagination made him fancy, in the play of heat quivering above the plain, the pebbles of his own dear Provence. But fearing all the dangers of this cruel mirage, he went down in the direction opposite to that which he had taken when he had climbed the hill the night before. Great was his joy on discovering a kind of grotto, naturally cut out of the enormous fragments of granite that formed the bottom of the hill. The remnants of a mat showed that this retreat had once been inhabited. Then, a few steps farther, he saw palm trees with a load of dates. Again the instinct which attaches man to life awoke within his heart. He now hoped to live until the passing of some Maugrabin; or perhaps he would soon hear the boom of cannon, for at that time Buonaparte was overrunning Egypt. Revived by this reflection, the Frenchman cut down a few bunches of ripe fruit, beneath whose weight the date trees seemed to bend, and felt sure, on tasting this unhoped-for manna, that the inhabitant of this grotto had cultivated the palm trees. The fresh and luscious substance of the date bore witness to his predecessor's care.

The Provençal passed suddenly from dark despair to well-nigh insane delight. He climbed the hill again; and spent the remainder of the day in cutting down a barren palm tree, which the night before had served him for shelter.

A vague remembrance made him think of the wild desert beasts; and, foreseeing that they might come to seek the spring which bubbled through the sand among the rocks, he resolved to secure himself against their visits by placing a barrier at the door of his hermitage. In spite of his exertions, in spite of the strength with which the fear of being eaten during sleep endued him, it was impossible for him to cut the palm to pieces in one day; but he contrived to bring it down. When, towards evening, the monarch of the desert fell, the thunder of its crash resounded far, as if the mighty Solitude had given forth a moan. The soldier shuddered as if he had heard a voice that prophesied misfortune. But like an heir who does not long bewail the death of a relation, he stripped the tree of the broad, long, green leaves, and used them to repair the mat on which he was about to lie. At length, wearied by the heat and by his labours, he fell asleep beneath the red roof of his murky grotto.

In the middle of the night he was disturbed by a strange noise. He sat up; in the profound silence he could hear a creature breathing – a savage respiration which resembled nothing human. Terror, intensified by darkness, silence, and the fancies of one suddenly awakened, froze his blood. He felt the sharp contraction of his scalp, when, as the pupils of his eyes dilated, he saw in the shadow two faint and yellow lights. At first he thought these lights were some reflection of his eyeballs, but soon, the clear brightness of the night helping him to distinguish objects in the grotto, he saw lying at two paces from him an enormous beast!

Was it a lion? – a tiger? – a crocodile? The Provençal was not sufficiently educated to know the species of his enemy, but his terror was all the greater; since his ignorance assisted his imagination. He bore the cruel torture of listening, of marking the caprices of this awful breathing, without losing a sound of it, or venturing to make the slightest movement. A smell as pungent as a fox's, but more penetrating, filled the grotto; and when it entered his nostrils his terror passed all bounds; he could no longer doubt the presence of the terrible companion whose royal den was serving him for bivouac. Presently the moon, now sinking, lighted up the den, and in the moon-rays gradually shone out a panther's spotted skin.

The lion of Egypt was sleeping, curled up like a great dog who is the peaceable possessor of a sumptuous kennel at a mansion door; its eyes, which had been opened for one moment, were now closed again. Its face was turned towards the Frenchman.

A thousand troubled thoughts passed through the mind of the panther's prisoner. At first he thought of shooting it; but there was not enough room between them to adjust his gun; the barrel would have reached beyond the animal. And what if he awoke it! This supposition made him motionless. Listening in the silence to the beating of his heart, he cursed the loud pulsations, fearing to disturb the sleep that gave him time to seek some means of safety. Twice he placed his hand upon his scimitar, with the intention of cutting off the head of his enemy; but the difficulty of cutting through the short, strong fur compelled him to abandon the idea. To fail was certain death. He preferred the odds of conflict, and determined to await the daybreak. And daylight was not long in coming. The Frenchman was able to examine the panther. Its muzzle was stained with blood.

'It has eaten plenty,' he reflected, without conjecturing that the feast might have been composed of human flesh; 'it will not be hungry when it wakes.'

It was a female. The fur upon her breast and thighs shone with whiteness. A number of little spots like velvet looked like charming bracelets around her paws. The muscular tail was also white, but tipped with black rings. The upper part of her coat, yellow as old gold, but very soft and smooth, bore these characteristic marks, shaded into the form of roses, which serve to distinguish the panther from the other species of the genus *Felis*. This fearful visitor was snoring tranquilly in an attitude as graceful as that of a kitten lying on the cushions of an ottoman. Her sinewy blood-stained paws, with powerful claws, were spread beyond her head, which rested on them, and from which stood out the thin, straight whiskers with a gleam like silver wires.

If she had been imprisoned in a cage, the Provençal would assuredly have admired the creature's grace, and the vivid contrasts of colour that gave her garment an imperial lustre; but at this moment he felt his sight grow dim at her sinister aspect. The presence of the panther, even sleeping, made him experience the effect which the magnetic eyes of the serpent are said to exercise upon the nightingale.

In the presence of this danger the courage of the soldier faltered, although without doubt it would have risen at the cannon's mouth. A desperate thought, however, filled his mind, and dried up at its source the chilly moisture which was rolling down his forehead. Acting as men do who, driven to extremities, at last defy their fate and nerve themselves to meet their doom, he saw a tragedy in this adventure, and resolved to play his part in it with honour to the last.

'Two days ago,' he argued with himself, 'the Arabs might have killed me.'

Considering himself as good as dead, he waited bravely, yet with restless curiosity, for the awaking of his enemy.

When the sun shone out, the panther opened her eyes suddenly; then she spread out her paws forcibly, as if to stretch them and get rid of cramp. Then she yawned, showing an alarming set ot teeth and an indented, rasp-like tongue. 'She is like a dainty lady!' thought the Frenchman, as he saw her rolling over with a gentle and coquettish movement. She licked off the blood that stained her paws and mouth, and rubbed her head with movements full of charm. 'That's it! Just beautify yourself a little!' the Frenchman said, his gaiety returning with his courage. 'Then we must say good morning!' And he took up the short dagger of which he had relieved the Maugrabins.

At this moment the panther turned her head towards the Frenchman, and looked at him fixedly, without advancing. The rigidity of those metallic eyes, and their insupportable brightness, made the Provençal shudder. The beast began to move towards him. He looked at her caressingly, and fixing her eyes as if to magnetise her, he let her come close up to him; then, with a soft and gentle gesture, he passed his hand along her body, from head to tail, scratching with his nails the flexible vertebrae that divide a panther's yellow back. The beast put up her tail with pleasure; her eyes grew softer; and when for the third time the Frenchman accomplished this self-interested piece of flattery, she broke into a purring like a cat. But this purr proceeded from a throat so deep and powerful that it re-echoed through the grotto like the peals of a cathedral organ. The Provençal realising the success of his caresses, redoubled them, until the imperious beauty was completely soothed and lulled.

When he felt sure that he had perfectly subdued the ferocity of his capricious companion, whose hunger had been satisfied so cruelly the night before, he got up to leave the grotto. The panther let him go; but when he had climbed the hill, she came bounding after him with the lightness of a sparrow hopping from branch to branch, and rubbed herself against the soldier's leg, arching her back after the fashion of a cat. Then looking at her guest with eyes whose brightness had grown less inflexible, she uttered that savage cry which naturalists have compared to the sound of a saw.

'What an exacting beauty!' cried the Frenchman, smiling. He set himself to play with her ears, to caress her body, and to scratch her head hard with his nails. Then, growing bolder with success, he tickled her skull with the point of his dagger, watching for the spot to strike her. But the hardness of the bones made him afraid of failing.

The sultana of the desert approved the action of her slave by raising her head, stretching her neck, and showing her delight by the quietness of her attitude. The Frenchman suddenly reflected that in order to assassinate this fierce princess with one blow he need only stab her in the neck. He had just raised his knife for the attempt, when the panther, with a graceful action, threw herself upon the ground before his feet, casting him from time to time a look in which, in spite of its ferocity of nature, there was a gleam of tenderness.

The poor Provençal, with his back against a palm tree, ate his dates, while he cast inquiring glances, now towards the desert for deliverers, now upon his terrible companion, to keep an eye upon her dubious clemency. Every time he threw away a date-stone, the panther fixed her eyes upon the spot with inconceivable mistrust. She scrutinised the Frenchman with a businesslike attention; but the examination seemed favourable, for when he finished his poor meal, she licked his boots, and with her rough, strong tongue removed the dust incrusted in their creases.

'But when she becomes hungry?' thought the Provençal.

Despite the shudder this idea caused him, the soldier began examining with curiosity the proportions of the panther, certainly one of the most beautiful specimens of her kind. She was three feet high and four feet long, without the tail. This powerful weapon, as round as a club, was nearly three feet long. The head – large as that of a lioness – was distinguished by an expression of rare delicacy; true, the cold cruelty of the tiger dominated, but there was also a resemblance to the features of a wily woman. In a word, the countenance of the solitary queen wore at this moment an expression of fierce gaiety, like that of Nero flushed with wine; she had quenched her thirst in blood, and now desired to play.

The soldier tried to come and go, and the panther let him, content to follow him with her eyes, but less after the manner of a faithful dog than of a great Angora cat, suspicious even of the movements of its master. When he turned round he saw beside the fountain the carcase of his horse; the panther had dragged the body all that distance. About two-thirds had been devoured. The sight reassured the Frenchman. He was thus easily able to explain the absence of the panther, and the respect which she had shown for him while he was sleeping.

This first piece of luck emboldened him about the future. He conceived the mad idea of setting up a pleasant household life, together with the panther, neglecting no means of pacifying her and of conciliating her good graces. He returned to her, and saw, to his delight, that she moved her tail with an almost imperceptible motion. Then he sat down beside her without fear, and began to play with her; he grasped her paws, her muzzle, pulled her ears, threw her over on her back, and vigorously scratched her warm and silky sides. She let him have his way, and when the soldier tried to smooth the fur upon her paws she carefully drew in her claws, which had the curve of a Damascus blade. The Frenchman, who kept one hand upon his dagger, was still thinking of plunging it into the body of the too-confining panther; but he feared lest she should strangle him in her last convulsions. And besides, within his heart there was a movement of remorse that warned him to respect an inoffensive creature. It seemed to him that he had found a friend in this vast desert. Involuntarily he called to mind a woman whom he once had loved, whom he sarcastically had nicknamed 'Mignonne,' from her jealousy, which was so fierce that during the whole time of their acquaintance he went in fear that she would stab him. This memory of his youth suggested the idea of calling the young panther by this name, whose lithe agility and grace he now admired with less terror.

Towards evening he had become so far accustomed to his perilous position, that he almost liked the hazard of it. At last his companion had got into the habit of looking at him when he called in a falsetto voice 'Mignonne.'

At sundówn Mignonne uttered several times a deep and melancholy cry.

'She has been properly brought up,' thought the light-hearted soldier; 'she says her prayers!' But it was, no doubt, her peaceful attitude which brought the jest into his mind.

'All right, my little pet; I will let you get to sleep first,' he said, relying on his legs to get away as soon as she was sleeping, and to seek some other shelter for the night.

The soldier waited with patience for the hour of flight, and when it came, set out full speed in the direction of the Nile. But he had only gone a quarter of a league across the sand when he heard the panther bounding after him, uttering at intervals that saw-like cry, more terrible even than the thudding of her leaps.

'Well!' he said to himself, 'she must have taken a fancy to me. Perhaps she has never yet met any one. It is flattering to be her first love!' At this moment the Frenchman fell into a shifting quicksand, so dangerous to the traveller in the desert, escape from which is hopeless. He felt that he was sinking; he gave a cry of terror. The panther seized him by the collar with her teeth, and springing backwards with stupendous vigour drew him from the gulf as if by magic.

'Ah! Mignonne!' cried the soldier, enthusiastically caressing her, 'we are friends now for life and death. But no tricks, eh?' and he retraced his steps.

Henceforth the desert was as though it had been peopled. It contained a being with whom he could converse, and whose ferocity had been softened for him, without his being able to explain so strange a friendship.

However great was his desire to keep awake and on his guard, he fell asleep. On awakening, Mignonne was no longer to be seen. He climbed the hill, and then perceived her afar off, coming along by leaps and bounds, according to the nature of these creatures, the extreme flexibility of whose vertebrae prevents their running.

Mignonne came up, her jaws besmeared with blood. She received the caresses of her companion with deep purrs of satisfaction. Her eyes, now full of softness, were turned, with even greater tenderness than the night before, to the Provençal, who spoke to her as to a pet.

'Ah! Beauty! you are a respectable young woman, are you not? You like petting, don't you? Are you not ashamed of yourself? You have been eating a Maugrabin! Well! they're animals, as you are. But don't you go and gobble up a Frenchman. If you do, I shall not love you!'

She played as a young pup plays with its master, letting him roll over, beat and pet her; and sometimes she would coax him to caress her with a movement of entreaty.

A few days passed thus. This companionship revealed to the Provençal the sublime beauties of the desert. From the moment when he found within it hours of fear and yet of calm, a sufficiency of food, and a living creature who absorbed his thoughts, his soul was stirred by new emotions. It was a life of contrasts. Solitude revealed to him her secrets, and involved him in her charm. He discovered in the rising and the setting of the sun a splendour hidden from the world of men. His frame quivered when he heard above his head the soft whirr of a bird's wings – rare wayfarer; or when he saw the clouds – those changeful, many-coloured voyagers – mingle in the depth of heaven. In the dead of night he studied the effects of the moon upon the sea of sand, which the simoom drove in ever-changing undulations. He lived with the Oriental day; he marvelled at its pomp and glory; and often, after having watched the grandeur of a tempest in the plain, in which the sands were whirled in dry red mists of deadly vapour, he beheld with ecstasy the coming on of night, for then there fell upon him the benignant coolness of the stars. He heard imaginary music in the sky. Solitude taught him all the bliss of reverie. He spent whole hours in calling trifles to remembrance, in comparing his past life with his strange present. To his panther he grew passionately attached, for he required an object of affection. Whether by a strong effort of his will he had really changed the character of his companion, or whether, thanks to the constant warfare of the desert, she found sufficient food, she showed no disposition to attack him, and at last, in her perfect tameness, he no longer felt the slightest fear.

He spent a great part of his time in sleeping, but ever, like a spider in its web, with mind alert, that he might not let deliverance escape him, should any chance to pass within the sphere described by the horizon. He had sacrificed his shirt to make a flag, which he had hoisted to the summit of a palm tree stripped of leaves. Taught by necessity, he had found the means to keep it spread by stretching it with sticks, lest the wind should fail to wave it at the moment when the hoped-for traveller might be travelling the waste of sand.

It was during the long hours when hope abandoned him that he amused himself with his companion. He had learnt to understand the different inflexions of her voice, and the expression of her glances; he had studied the varying changes of the spots that starred her robe of gold. Mignonne no longer growled, even when he seized her by the tuft with which her terrible tail ended, to count the black and white rings which adorned it, and which glittered in the sun like precious gems. It delighted him to watch the delicate soft lines of her snowy breast and graceful head. But above all when she was gambolling in her play he watched her with delight, for the agility, the youthfulness of all her movements filled him with an ever-fresh surprise. He admired her suppleness in leaping, climbing, gliding, pressing close against him, swaying, rolling over, crouching for a bound. But however swift her spring, however slippery the block of granite, she would stop short, without motion, at the sound of the word 'Mignonne!'

One day, in the most dazzling sunshine, an enormous bird was hovering in the air. The Provençal left his panther to examine this new visitor; but after waiting for a moment the deserted sultana uttered a hoarse growl.

'Blessed if I don't believe that she is jealous!' he exclaimed, perceiving that her eyes were once more hard and rigid. 'A woman's soul has passed into her body, that is certain!'

The eagle disappeared in air, while he admired afresh the rounded back and graceful outlines of the panther. She was as pretty as a woman. The blonde fur blended in its delicate gradations into the dull white colour of the thighs. The brilliant sunshine made this vivid gold, with spots of brown, take on a lustre indescribable. The Provençal and the panther looked at one another understandingly; the beauty of the desert quivered when she felt the nails of her admirer on her skull. Her eyes gave forth a flash like lightning, and then she closed them hard.

'She *has* a soul,' he cried, as he beheld the desert queen in her repose, golden as the sands, white as their blinding lustre, and, like them, fiery and alone.

'Well?' she said to me, 'I have read your pleading on behalf of animals. But what was the end of these two persons so well made to understand each other?'

'Ah! They ended as all great passions end – through a misunderstanding. Each thinks the other guilty of a falsity, each is too proud for explanation, and obstinacy brings about a rupture.'

'And sometimes in the happiest moments,' she said, 'a look, an exclamation, is enough! Well, what was the end of the story?'

'That is difficult to tell, but you will understand what the old fellow had confided to me, when, finishing his bottle of champagne, he exclaimed, "I don't know how I hurt her, but she turned on me like mad, and with her sharp teeth seized my thigh. The action was not savage, but fancying that she meant to kill me I plunged my dagger into her neck. She rolled over with a cry that froze my blood; she looked at me in her last struggles without anger. I would have given everything on earth, even my cross – which then I had not won – to bring her back to life. It was as if I had slain a human being. And the soldiers who had seen my flag, and who were hastening to my succour, found me bathed in tears."

'"Well, sir," he went on, after a moment's silence, "since then I have been through the wars in Germany, Spain, Russia, France; I have dragged my carcase round the world; but there is nothing like the desert in my eyes! Ah! it is beautiful – superb!"

'"What did you feel there?" I inquired of him.

'"Oh! that I cannot tell you. Besides, I do not always regret my panther and my clump of palm trees. I must be sad at heart for that. But mark my words. In the desert there is everything and there is nothing."

'"Explain yourself."

'"Well!" he continued, with a gesture of impatience, "it is God without man."'

AN EPISODE OF THE REIGN OF TERROR

AN EPISODE OF THE REIGN OF TERROR

About eight o'clock on the evening of January 22, 1793, an aged woman was coming down the sharp descent of the Faubourg Saint-Martin that ends in front of the church of Saint-Laurent. Snow had fallen so heavily all day long that hardly a footfall could be heard. The streets were deserted. Fears that the silence around naturally enough inspired were increased by all the terror under which France was then groaning. So the old lady had thus far met with no one else. Her sight, which had long been failing, did not enable her to distinguish far off by the light of the street lamps some passers-by moving like scattered shadows in the huge thoroughfare of the Faubourg. She went on bravely all alone in the midst of this solitude, as if her age were a talisman that could be relied on to preserve her from any mishap.

When she had passed the Rue des Morts she thought she perceived the heavy, firm tread of a man walking behind her. It occurred to her that it was not the first time she had heard this sound. She was alarmed at the idea that she was being followed, and she tried to walk faster in order to reach a fairly well-lighted shop, in the hope that, in the light it gave, she would be able to put to the test the suspicions that had taken possession of her.

As soon as she was within the circle of light projected horizontally by the shop-front, she quickly turned her head and caught a glimpse of a human form in the foggy darkness. This vague glimpse was enough for her. She tottered for a moment under the shock of terror that overwhelmed her, for she no longer doubted that she had been followed by the stranger from the first step she had taken outside her lodging. The longing to escape from a spy gave her strength. Without being able to think of what she was doing, she began to run – as if she could possibly get away from a man who must necessarily be much more agile than herself.

After running for a few minutes she reached a confectioner's shop, entered it, and fell, rather than sat, down upon a chair that stood in front of the counter. Even while she was raising the creaking latch, a young woman, who was busy with some embroidery, raised her eyes, and through the small panes of the half-window in the shop door recognised the old-fashioned violet silk mantle in which the old lady was wrapped. She hurriedly opened a drawer as if looking for something she was to hand over to her.

It was not only by her manner and the look on her face that the young woman showed she was anxious to get rid of the stranger without delay, as if her visitor were one of those there was no pleasure in seeing; but, besides this, she allowed an expression of impatience to escape her on finding that the drawer was empty. Then, without looking at the lady, she turned suddenly from the counter, went towards the back shop, and called her husband, who at once made his appearance.

'Whatever have you put away. . . ?' she asked of him with an air of mystery, without finishing her question, but calling his attention to the old lady with a glance of her eyes.

Although the confectioner could see nothing but the immense black silk bonnet, trimmed with bows of velvet ribbon, that formed the strange visitor's headgear, he left the shop again, after having cast at his wife a look that seemed to say, 'Do you think I would leave *that* in your counter. . . ?'

Surprised at the motionless silence of the old lady, the shopwoman turned and approached her, and as she looked at her she felt herself inspired with an impulse of compassion, perhaps not unmingled with curiosity. Although the woman's complexion showed an habitual pallor, like that of one who makes a practice of secret austerities, it was easy to see that a recent emotion had brought an unusual paleness to her face. Her headdress was so arranged as to conceal her hair. No doubt it was white with age, for there were no marks on the upper part of her dress to show that she used hair powder. The complete absence of ornament lent to her person an air of religious severity. Her features had a grave, stately look. In these old times the manners and habits of people of quality were so different from those of other classes of society, that it was easy to distinguish one of noble birth. So the young woman felt convinced that the stranger was a *ci-devant*, an ex-aristocrat, and that she had belonged to the court.

'Madame . . .' she said to her with involuntary respect, forgetting that such a title was now forbidden.

The old lady did not reply. She kept her eyes fixed on the window of the shop, as if she could distinguish some fearful object in that direction.

'What is the matter, citizeness?' asked the shopkeeper, who had returned almost immediately.

And the citizen–confectioner roused the lady from her reverie by offering her a little cardboard box wrapped in blue paper.

'Nothing, nothing, my friends,' she answered in a sweet voice. She raised her eyes to the confectioner's face as if to give him a look of thanks, but seeing the red cap on his head, she uttered a cry: 'Ah, you have betrayed me!'

The young woman and her husband replied by a gesture of horror at the thought, which made the stranger blush, perhaps at having suspected them, perhaps with pleasure.

'Pardon me,' she said, with childlike gentleness. Then, taking a *louis d'or* from her pocket, she offered it to the confectioner: 'Here is the price we agreed on,' she added.

There is a poverty that the poor readily recognise. The confectioner and his wife looked at one another, silently turning each other's attention to the old lady, while both formed one common thought. This *louis d'or* must be her last. The lady's hands trembled as she offered the piece of money, she looked at it with a sadness that had no avarice in it, but she seemed to realise the full extent of the sacrifice she made. Starvation and misery were as plainly marked on her face as the lines that told of fear and of habits of asceticism. In her dress there were traces of old magnificence. It was of worn-out silk. Her mantle was neat though threadbare, with some carefully mended lace upon it. In a word, it was a case of wealth the worse for wear. The people of the shop, hesitating between sympathy and self-interest, began by trying to satisfy their consciences with words:

'But, citizeness, you seem to be very weak —'

'Would Madame like to take something?' said the woman, cutting her husband short.

'We have some very good soup,' added the confectioner.

'It is so cold tonight. Perhaps Madame has had a chill while walking? But you can rest here and warm yourself for a while.'

'We are not as black as the devil!' exclaimed the confectioner.

Won by the tone of kindness that found expression in the words of the charitable shopkeepers, the lady let them know she had been followed by a stranger, and that she was afraid to go back alone to her lodgings.

'Is that all?' replied the man in the red cap. 'Wait a little, citizeness.'

He gave the *louis d'or* to his wife. . . . Then moved by that sort of gratitude that finds its way into the heart of a dealer when he has got an exorbitant price for some merchandise of trifling value, he went and put on his National Guards' uniform, took his hat, belted on his sword, and reappeared as an armed man. But his wife had had time to reflect. In her heart, as in so many more, reflection closed the open hand of benevolence. Anxious and fearful of seeing her husband involved in some bad business, the confectioner's wife tried to pull him by the skirt of his coat and stop him. But obeying his own charitable feelings the good fellow offered at once to escort the old lady.

'It seems that the man the citizeness is afraid of is still prowling about in front of our shop,' said the young woman excitedly.

'I am afraid he is,' put in the lady naïvely.

'What if he were a spy? . . . if there were some plot? . . . Don't go, and take back that box from her. . . .'

These words, whispered in the ear of the confectioner by his wife, froze the sudden courage that had inspired him.

'Well, I'll just say a few words to him, and rid you of him soon enough,' exclaimed the shopkeeper, as he opened the door and slipped hurriedly out.

The old lady, passive as a child and almost stupefied by her fear, sat down again on the chair. The good shopkeeper was soon back. His face, naturally ruddy enough and further reddened by his oven fire, had suddenly become pallid. He was a prey to such terror that his legs shook and his eyes looked like those of a drunken man.

'Do you want to get our heads cut off, you wretch of an aristocrat?' he cried out in a fury. 'Come, show us your heels, and don't let us see you again, and don't reckon on my supplying you with materials for your plots!'

As he ended, the confectioner made an attempt to take back from the old lady the little box which she had put into one of her pockets. But hardly had his bold hands touched her dress, than the stranger, preferring to risk herself amid the perils of the street without any other protector but God, rather than to lose what she had just bought, regained all the agility of youth. She rushed to the door, opened it briskly, and vanished from the sight of wife and husband as they stood trembling and astonished.

As soon as the stranger was outside she started off at a rapid walk. But her strength soon began to desert her, and she heard the spy, who had so pitilessly followed her, making the snow crackle as he crushed it with his heavy tread. She had to stop. He stopped. She did not dare to address him, or even to look at him – it might be on account of the fear that had seized upon her, or because she could not think what to say. Then she went on again walking slowly.

The man also slackened his pace so as to remain always just at the distance that enabled him to keep her in sight. He seemed to be the very shadow of the old woman. Nine o'clock struck as the silent pair once more passed by the church of Saint-Laurent.

It is a part of the nature of all minds, even of the weakest, to find a feeling of calm succeed to any violent agitation, for if our feelings are infinite, our organism has its limits. So the stranger, finding that her supposed persecutor did her no harm, was inclined to see in him some unknown friend, who was anxious to protect her. She summed up in her mind all the circumstances that had attended the appearance of the stranger, as if seeking for some plausible motives for this consoling opinion, and was then satisfied to recognise on his part a friendly rather than an evil purpose. Forgetful of the alarm, which this man had so short a time ago caused the confectioner, she now went on with a firm step into the upper part of the Faubourg Saint-Martin.

After walking for half an hour she came to a house situated near the point where the street, which leads to the Pantin barrier, branches off from the main line of the Faubourg. Even at the present day the neighbourhood is still one of the loneliest in all Paris. A north-east wind blowing over the Buttes Chaumont and Belleville whistled between the houses, or rather the cottages, scattered about this almost uninhabited valley, in which the enclosures were formed of fences built up of earth and old bones. The desolate place seemed to be the natural refuge of misery and despair.

The man, all eagerness in the pursuit of this poor creature, who was so bold as to traverse these silent streets in the night, seemed struck by the spectacle that presented itself to his gaze. He stood still, full of thought, in a hesitating attitude, in the feeble light of a street lamp, the struggling rays of which could hardly penetrate the fog. Fear seemed to sharpen the sight of the old lady, who thought she saw something of evil omen in the looks of the stranger. She felt her terror reawakening, and took advantage of the seeming hesitation that had brought the man to a standstill to slip through a shadow to the door of a solitary house; she pushed back a spring latch, and disappeared in an instant like a ghost upon the stage.

The unknown man, without moving from where he stood, kept his eyes fixed on the house, the appearance of which was fairly typical of that of the wretched dwelling-places of this suburb of Paris. The tumble-down hovel was built of bricks covered with a coat of yellow plaster, so full of cracks that one feared to see the whole fall down in a heap of ruins before the least effort of the wind. There were three windows to each floor, and their frames, rotten with damp and warped by the action of the sun, suggested that the cold must penetrate freely into the rooms. The lonely house looked like some old tower that time has forgotten to destroy. A feeble gleam lit up the warped and crooked window-sashes of the garret window, that showed up the roof of this poor edifice, while all the rest of the house was in complete darkness.

Not without difficulty the old woman climbed the rough and clumsy stair, in ascending which one had to lean on a rope that took the place of a hand-rail. She gave a low knock at the door of the garret room, and hurriedly took her seat on a chair, which an old man offered to her.

'Hide yourself! hide yourself!' she said to him, 'though we so seldom go out, our doings are known, our steps are spied upon. . . .'

'Is there anything new then?' asked another old woman, who was seated near the fire.

'That man, who has been prowling round the house since yesterday, followed me this evening. . . .'

At these words the three inmates of the hovel looked at each other, while they showed on their faces signs of serious alarm. Of the three the old man was the least agitated, perhaps because he was the most in danger. Under the weight of a great misfortune, or under the pressure of persecution, a brave man begins, so to say, by making the complete sacrifice of himself. He counts each day as one more victory won over fate. The looks of the two women fixed upon this old man made it easy to see that he was the one object of their keen anxiety.

'Why lose our trust in God, my sisters?' he said in a voice low but full of fervour; 'we sang His praises in the midst of the cries of the murderers and of the dying at the convent of the Carmelites. If He willed that I should be saved from that butchery, it was no doubt to preserve me for some destiny that I must accept without a murmur. God guards His own, and He can dispose of them according to His will. It is of yourselves, and not of me, that we must think.'

'No,' said one of the old women, 'what are our lives compared to that of a priest?'

'Once I saw myself outside of the Abbey of Chelles, I considered myself as a dead woman,' said one of the two nuns – the one who had remained in the house.

'Here are the altar breads,' said the other, who had just come in, offering the little box to the priest. 'But . . .' she cried out, 'I hear footsteps on the stairs!'

All three listened. . . . The sound ceased.

'Do not be alarmed,' said the priest, 'if someone tries to get to see you. A person on whose good faith we can depend must by this time have taken all necessary steps to cross the frontier, in order to come here for the letters I have written to the Duc de Langeais and the Marquis de Beauséant, asking them to see what can be done to take you away from this wretched country, and the suffering and death that await you here.'

'You are not going with us then?' exclaimed the two nuns in gentle protest, and with a look of something like despair.

'My place is where there are still victims,' was the priest's simple reply.

They were silent, and gazed at their protector with reverent admiration.

'Sister Martha,' he said, addressing the nun who had gone to get the altar breads, 'this envoy of ours should answer "*Fiat voluntas*" to the password "*Hosanna.*"'

'There is someone on the stair!' exclaimed the other nun; and she opened a hiding-place constructed in the roof.

This time, in the deep silence, it was easy to catch the sound of the footsteps of some man, re-echoing on the stairs that were rough with lumps of hardened mud. The priest with some difficulty huddled himself into a kind of cupboard, and the nun threw some old clothes over him.

'You can shut the door,' he said in a smothered voice.

The priest was hardly hidden away, when three knocks at the door made both the good women start. They were exchanging looks of inquiry without daring to utter a word. Both seemed to be about sixty years of age. Separated from the world for some forty years, they were like plants that are so used to the air of a hothouse that they die if one takes them out. Accustomed as they were to the life of the convent they had no idea of anything else. One morning their cloister had been broken open, and they had shuddered at finding themselves free. It is easy to imagine the state of nervous weakness the events of the Revolution had produced in their innocent minds. Unable to reconcile the mental habits of the cloister with the difficulties of life, and not fully understanding the circumstances in which they were placed, they were like children of whom every care had been taken till now, and who, suddenly deprived of their mother's care, pray instead of weeping. So face to face with the danger which they now saw before them, they remained silent and passive, knowing of no other defence but Christian resignation.

The man who had asked for admittance interpreted this silence in his own way. He opened the door and suddenly appeared in the room. The two nuns shuddered as they recognised the man who for some time had been prowling around their house and making inquiries about them. They remained motionless, looking at him with the anxious curiosity of untaught children who stare in silence at a stranger.

The man was tall in stature and heavily built. But there was nothing in his attitude, his general appearance, or the expression of his face to suggest that he was a bad character. Like the nuns, he kept quite still, and slowly cast his eyes round the room he had entered.

Two straw mats unrolled on the floor served for beds for the nuns. There was a table in the middle of the room, and there stood on it a brass candlestick, some plates, three knives, and a round loaf of bread. There was a very small fire in the grate. A few pieces of wood heaped up in a corner were a further sign of the poverty of these two recluses. One could see that the roof was in a bad state, for the walls, covered with a coat of very old paint, were stained with brown streaks that showed where the rain had leaked through. A reliquary, rescued no doubt from the sack of the Abbey of Chelles, served as an ornament to the mantelpiece. Three chairs, two boxes, and a shabby chest of drawers completed the furniture of the room. A door near the fireplace suggested that there was a second room beyond.

The individual who had in such an alarming way introduced himself to this poor household had soon taken mental note of all the contents of the little room. A feeling of pity could be traced upon his countenance, and he cast a kindly look upon the two women, and appeared to be at least as much embarrassed as they were. The strange silence that all three had kept so far did not long continue, for at last the stranger realised the timidity and inexperience of the two poor creatures, and said to them in a voice that he tried to make as gentle as possible:

'I do not come here as an enemy, citizenesses . . .' He stopped, as if recovering himself, and went on:

'Sisters, if any misfortune comes your way, believe me I have no part in it. . . . I have a favour to ask of you.'

They still kept silence.

'If I am troubling you, if . . . if I am causing you pain, say so freely . . . and I will go away; but be assured that I am entirely devoted to you; that if there is any kindness I can do to you, you can claim it from me without fear; and that I am perhaps the only one who is above the law, now that there is no longer a king. . . .'

There was such an air of truth in his words, that Sister Agatha – she of the two nuns who belonged to the noble family of Langeais, and whose manners seemed to indicate that in old times she had known the splendours of festive society and had breathed the air of the court – pointed with an alert movement to one of the chairs as if asking the visitor to be seated. The stranger showed something of pleasure mingled with sadness as he understood this gesture, but before taking the chair he waited till both the worthy ladies were seated.

'You have given a refuge here,' he continued, 'to a venerable priest, one of those who refused the oath, and who had a miraculous escape from the massacre at the Carmelites. . . .'

'*Hosanna!*' . . . said Sister Agatha, interrupting the stranger, and looking at him with anxious curiosity.

'I don't think that is his name,' he replied.

'But, sir, we have no priest here,' said Sister Martha, eagerly.

'If that is so, you ought to be more careful and prudent,' answered the stranger in a gentle tone, as he stretched out his hand to the table and took a breviary from it. 'I don't suppose you know Latin, and . . .'

He said no more, for the extraordinary emotion depicted on the faces of the two poor nuns made him fear that he had gone too far. They were trembling, and their eyes filled with tears.

'Don't be alarmed,' he said in a voice that seemed all sincerity, 'I know the name of your guest, and your own names too, and for the last three days I have been aware of your distress and of your devoted care for the venerable Abbé de . . .'

'Hush!' said Sister Agatha in her simplicity, putting a finger to her lips.

'You see, Sister, that if I had had in my mind the horrible idea of betraying you, I could have done so already, again and again. . . .'

Hearing these words, the priest extricated himself from his prison and came out again into the room.

'I could not possibly believe, sir,' he said to the stranger, 'that you were one of our persecutors, and I trust myself to you. What do you want of me?'

The holy confidence of the priest, the nobility of mind that showed itself in his every look, would have disarmed even assassins. The mysterious man, whose coming had caused such excitement in this scene of resigned misery, gazed for a moment at the group formed by the three others; then, taking a tone in which there was no longer any hesitation, he addressed the priest in these words:

'Father, I came to ask you to say a mass for the dead, for the repose of the soul . . . of one . . . of a sacred personage, whose body will never be laid to rest in consecrated ground. . . .'

The priest gave an involuntary shudder. The nuns, who did not yet understand to whom it was the stranger alluded, sat in an attitude of curiosity, their heads stretched forwards, their faces turned towards the two who were speaking together. The priest looked closely at the stranger, on whose face there was an unmistakable expression of anxiety, and also of earnest entreaty.

'Well,' replied the priest, 'come back this evening at midnight, and I shall be ready to celebrate the only rites for the dead that we may be able to offer up in expiation for the crime of which you speak. . . .'

The stranger started, but it seemed that some deep and soothing satisfaction was triumphing over his secret sorrow. After having respectfully saluted the priest and the two holy women, he took his departure, showing a kind of silent gratitude which was understood by these three generous souls.

About two hours after this scene the stranger returned, knocked softly at the door of the garret, and was admitted by Mademoiselle de Beauséant, who led him into the inner room of this poor place of refuge, where everything had been made ready for the ceremony.

Between two chimney-shafts that passed up through the room the nuns had placed the old chest of drawers, the antiquated outlines of which were hidden by a magnificent altar frontal of green watered silk. A large crucifix of ivory and ebony hung on the yellow-washed wall, contrasting so strongly with the surrounding bareness that the eye could not fail to be drawn to it. Four slender little tapers, which the sisters had succeeded in fixing on this improvised altar, by attaching them to it with sealing-wax, threw out a dim light, that was hardly reflected by the wall. This feeble illumination barely gave light to the rest of the room; but, as it thus shone only on the sacred objects, it seemed like a light sent down from heaven on this unadorned altar. The floor was damp. The roof, which slanted down sharply on two sides, as is usual in garret rooms, had some cracks in it through which came the night wind – icy cold.

Nothing could be more devoid of all pomp, and nevertheless there was perhaps never anything more solemn than this mournful ceremony. A profound silence, in which one could have heard the least sound uttered on the highway outside, lent a kind of sombre majesty to the midnight scene. Finally, the greatness of the action itself contrasted so strongly with the poverty of its surroundings that the result was a feeling of religious awe.

On each side of the altar the two aged nuns knelt on the tiled floor without taking any notice of its deadly dampness, and united their prayers with those of the priest, who, robed in his sacerdotal vestments, placed on the altar a chalice of gold adorned with precious stones, a consecrated vessel that had been saved no doubt from the pillage of the Abbey of Chelles. Besides this chalice, a token of royal munificence, the wine and water destined for the Holy Sacrifice stood ready in two glasses, such as one would hardly have found in the poorest inn. For want of a missal the priest had placed a small prayer-book on the corner of the altar. An ordinary plate had been prepared for the washing of the hands, in this case hands all innocent and free from blood. There was the contrast of littleness with immensity; of poverty with noble sublimity; of what was meant for profane uses with what was consecrated to God.

The stranger knelt devoutly between the two nuns. But suddenly, as he noticed that, having no other means of marking that this was a mass offered for the dead, the priest had placed a knot of crape on the crucifix and on the base of the chalice, thus putting holy things in mourning, the stranger's mind was so mastered by some recollection that drops of sweat stood out upon his broad forehead. The four silent actors in the scene looked at each other mysteriously. Then their souls, acting and reacting on each other, inspired with one common thought, united them in devout sympathy. It seemed as if their minds had evoked the presence of the martyr whose remains the quick-lime had burned away, and that his shade was present with them in all its kingly majesty. They were celebrating a requiem without the presence of the body of the departed. Under the disjointed laths and tiles of the roof four Christians were about to intercede with God for a King of France, and perform his obsequies though there was no coffin before the altar. There was the purest of devoted love, an act of wondrous loyalty performed without a touch of self-consciousness. No doubt, in the eyes of God, it was like the gift of the glass of water that ranks with the highest of virtues. All the monarchy was there, finding voice in the prayers of a priest and two poor women; but perhaps the Revolution too was represented by that man, whose face showed too much remorse to leave any doubt that he was fulfilling a duty inspired by deep repentance.

Before he pronounced the Latin words, *Introibo ad altare Dei*, the priest, as if by an inspiration from on high, turned to the three who were with him as the representatives of Christian France, and said to them, as though to banish from their sight all the misery of the garret room:

'We are about to enter into the sanctuary of God!'

At these words, uttered with deep devotion, a holy awe took possession of the stranger and the two nuns. Under the vast arches of St Peter's at Rome these Christians could not have realised the majesty of God's Presence more plainly than in that refuge of misery; so true is it that between Him and man all outward things seem useless, and His greatness comes from Himself alone. The stranger showed a really fervent devotion. So the same feelings united the prayers of these four servants of God and the King. The sacred words sounded like a heavenly music in the midst of the silence. There was a moment when the unknown man could not restrain his tears. It was at the *Pater Noster*, when the priest added this prayer in Latin which no doubt the stranger understood:

'*Et remitte scelus regicidis sicut Ludovicus eis remisit semetipse*
(And forgive their crime to the regicides, as Louis himself
forgave them.)'

The nuns saw two large tear-drops making lines of moisture
down the strong face of the unknown, and falling to the floor.

The Office for the Dead was recited. The *Domine salvum fac
regem*, chanted in a low voice, touched the hearts of these
faithful Royalists, who thought how the child King, for
whom at that moment they were imploring help of the Most
High, was a captive in the hands of his enemies. The stranger
shuddered as he remembered that perhaps a fresh crime might
be committed, in which he would no doubt be forced to have
a share.

When the Office for the Dead was ended, the priest made a
sign to the two nuns and they withdrew. As soon as he found
himself alone with the stranger, he went towards him with a
sad and gentle air, and said to him in a fatherly voice:

'My son, if you have imbrued your hands in the blood of
the martyr King, confide in me. There is no fault that is not
blotted out in God's eyes by a repentance as sincere and as
touching as yours appears to be.'

At the first words uttered by the priest the stranger gave
way to an involuntary movement of alarm. But he recovered
his self-control, and looked calmly at the astonished priest.

'Father,' he said to him, in a voice that showed evident signs
of emotion, 'no one is more innocent than I am of the blood
that has been shed. . . .'

'It is my duty to take your word for it,' said the priest.

There was a pause, during which once more he looked
closely at his penitent. Then, persisting in taking him for one
of those timid members of the National Convention who
abandoned to the executioner a sacred and inviolable head in
order to save their own, he spoke once more in a grave tone:

'Consider, my son, that in order to be guiltless of this great
crime it does not suffice merely to have had no direct
co-operation in it. Those who, although they could have
defended the king, left their swords in their scabbards, will
have a very heavy account to render to the King of
Heaven. . . . Oh, yes!' added the old priest, shaking his head
expressively from side to side. 'Yes, very heavy! . . . for in

standing idle, they have made themselves the involuntary accomplices of this awful misdeed.'

'Do you think,' asked the man, as if struck with horror, 'that even an indirect participation in it will be punished? . . . Are we then to take it that, say, a soldier who was ordered to keep the ground at the scaffold is guilty? . . .'

The priest hesitated. Pleased at the dilemma in which he had put this Puritan of Royalism, by placing him between the doctrine of passive obedience, which, according to the partisans of the monarchy, must be the essence of the military code, and the equally important doctrine which was the sanction of the respect due to the person of the King, the stranger eagerly accepted the priest's hesitation as indicating a favourable solution of the doubts that seemed to harass him. Then, in order not to give the venerable theologian further time for reflection, he said to him:

'I would be ashamed to offer you any honorarium for the funeral service you have just celebrated for the repose of the soul of the King, and to satisfy my own conscience. One can only pay the price of what is inestimable by offering that which is also beyond price. Will you therefore condescend, sir, to accept the gift I make you of a sacred relic. . . . Perhaps the day will come when you will understand its value.'

As he ceased speaking, the stranger held out to the priest a little box that was extremely light. The latter took it in his hands automatically, so to say, for the solemnity of the words of this man, the tone in which he spoke, the reverence with which he handled the box, had plunged him into a reverie of deep astonishment. Then they returned to the room where the two nuns were waiting for them.

'You are,' said the stranger to them, 'in a house the proprietor of which, the plasterer, Mucius Scaevola, who lives in the first storey, is famous in the quarter for his patriotism. But all the same he is secretly attached to the Bourbons. Formerly he was a huntsman to Monseigneur the Prince de Conti, and he owes his fortune to him. By staying here you are safer than anywhere else in France. Remain here, therefore. Certain pious souls will provide for your needs, and you can wait without danger for less evil times. A year hence, on January 21st' (as he pronounced these last words, he could not conceal an involuntary start), 'if this poor place is still your refuge, I shall come back to assist once more with you at a mass of expiation.'

He stopped without further explanation. He saluted the silent inhabitants of the garret, took in with a last look the signs that told of their poverty, and left the room.

For the two simple nuns such an adventure had all the interest of a romance. So when the venerable abbé had told them of the mysterious present so solemnly made to him by this man, they placed the box on the table, and the feeble light of the candle, shining on the three anxious faces, showed on all of them a look of indescribable curiosity. Mademoiselle de Langeais opened the box, and found in it a handkerchief of fine cambric soiled with perspiration. As they unfolded it they saw spots on it.

'They are blood stains,' said the priest.

'It is marked with the royal crown!' exclaimed the other sister.

With a feeling of horror the two sisters dropped the precious relic. For these two simple souls the mystery that surrounded the stranger had become something inexplicable. And, as for the priest, from that day he did not even attempt to find an explanation of it in his own mind.

It was not long before the three prisoners realised that notwithstanding the Terror an invisible hand was stretched out to protect them. At first firewood and provisions were sent in for them. Then the two nuns guessed that a woman was associated with their protector, for they were sent linen and clothes that would make it possible for them to go out without attracting attention by the aristocratic fashion of the dress they had been forced to wear till then. Finally Mucius Scaevola provided them with two 'civic cards,' certificates of good citizenship. Often by roundabout ways they received warnings, that were necessary for the safety of the priest, and they recognised that these friendly hints came so opportunely that they could only emanate from someone who was initiated into the secrets of the state. Notwithstanding the famine from which Paris was suffering, the refugees found rations of white bread left regularly at their garret door by invisible hands. However, they thought they could identify in Mucius

Scaevola the mysterious agent of this beneficence, which was always as ingenious as it was well directed.

The noble refugees in the garret could have no doubt but that their protector was the same person who had come to assist at the mass of expiation on the night of January 22nd, 1793. He thus became the object of a very special regard on the part of all three. They hoped in him only, lived only thanks to him. They had added special prayers for him to their devotions; morning and night these pious souls offered up petitions for his welfare, for his prosperity, for his salvation. They begged God to remove all temptations from him, to deliver him from his enemies, and to give him a long and peaceful life. Their gratitude was thus, so to say, daily renewed, but was inevitably associated with a feeling of curiosity that became keener as day after day went by.

The circumstances that had attended the appearance of the stranger were the subject of their conversations. They formed a thousand conjectures with regard to him, and it was a fresh benefit to them of another kind that he thus served to distract their minds from other thoughts. They were quite determined that on the night when, according to his promise, he would come back to celebrate the mournful anniversary of the death of Louis XVI, they would not let him go without establishing more friendly relations with him.

The night to which they had looked forward so impatiently came at last. At midnight the heavy footsteps of the unknown resounded on the old wooden stair. The room had been made ready to receive him; the altar was prepared. This time the sisters opened the door before he reached it, and both hastened to show a light on the staircase. Mademoiselle de Langeais even went down a few steps in order the sooner to see their benefactor.

'Come,' she said to him in a voice trembling with affection, 'come . . . you are expected.'

The man raised his head, and without replying cast a gloomy look at the nun. She felt as if a mantle of ice had fallen around her, and kept silence. At the sight of him the feeling of gratitude and of curiosity died out in all their hearts. He was perhaps less cold, less taciturn, less terrible than he appeared to these souls, whom the excitement of their feelings disposed to

a, warm and friendly welcome. The three poor prisoners
realised that the man wished to remain a stranger to them, and
they accepted the situation.

The priest thought that he noticed a smile, that was at once
repressed, play upon the lips of the unknown, when he
remarked the preparations that had been made for his recep-
tion. He heard mass and prayed. But then he went away after
having declined, with a few words of polite refusal, the
invitation that Mademoiselle de Langeais offered him to share
with them the little supper that had been made ready.

After the 9th Thermidor – (the fall of Robespierre) – both
the nuns and the Abbé de Marolles were able to go about in
Paris without incurring the least danger. The old priest's first
excursion was to a perfumer's shop at the sign of the *Reine des
Fleurs*, kept by Citizen Ragon and his wife, formerly
perfumers to the court, who had remained faithful to the royal
family. The Vendéans made use of them as their agents for
corresponding with the exiled princes and the royalist
committee at Paris. The abbé, dressed as the times required,
was standing on the doorstep of the shop, which was situated
between the Church of Saint Roch and the Rue des Frondeurs,
when a crowd, which filled all the Rue Saint-Honoré,
prevented him from going out.

'What is the matter?' he asked Madame Ragon.

'It's nothing,' she replied. 'It's the cart with the executioner
on the way to the Place Louis XV. Ah! we saw it often enough
last year. But today, four days after the anniversary of January
21st, one can watch that terrible procession go by without
feeling displeasure.'

'Why?' said the abbé, 'it is not Christian of you to talk thus.'

'But it's the execution of the accomplices of Robespierre.
They did their best to save themselves, but they are going in
their turn where they sent so many innocent people!'

The crowd was pouring past like a flood. The Abbé de
Marolles, yielding to an impulse of curiosity, saw, standing
erect on the cart, the man who three days before had come to
hear his mass.

'Who is that?' he said, 'the man who . . .'

'It's the hangman,' replied Monsieur Ragon, giving the
executioner the name he bore under the monarchy.

'My dear, my dear,' cried out Madame Ragon, 'Monsieur l'Abbé is dying!'

And the old lady seized a bottle of smelling salts with which to revive the aged priest from a fainting fit.

'No doubt,' he said, 'what he gave me was the handkerchief with which the King wiped his forehead as he went to martyrdom. . . . Poor man! . . . The steel blade had a heart when all France was heartless! . . .'

The perfumers thought that the poor priest was raving.

THE CONSCRIPT

THE CONSCRIPT

One evening in the month of November 1793 the principal people of Carentan were gathered in the salon of Madame de Dey, at whose house the assembly was held daily. Some circumstances which would not have attracted attention in a large city, but which were certain to cause a flutter in a small one, lent to this customary meeting an unusual degree of interest. Two days before, Madame de Dey had closed her door to her guests, whom she had also excused herself from receiving on the preceding day, on the pretext of an indisposition. In ordinary times, these two occurrences would have produced the same effect in Carentan that the closing of all the theatres would produce in Paris. In those days existence was to a certain extent incomplete. And in 1793 the conduct of Madame de Dey might have had the most deplorable results. The slightest venturesome proceeding almost always became a question of life or death for the nobles of that period.

In order to understand the intense curiosity and the narrow-minded cunning which enlivened the Norman countenances of all those people during the evening, but especially in order that we may share the secret anxiety of Madame de Dey, it is necessary to explain the rôle that she played at Carentan. As the critical position in which she found herself at that moment was undoubtedly identical with that of many people during the Revolution, the sympathies of more than one reader will give the needed touch of colour to this narrative.

Madame de Dey, the widow of a lieutenant-general and chevalier of the Orders, had left the court at the beginning of the emigration. As she possessed considerable property in the neighbourhood of Carentan, she had taken refuge there, hoping that the influence of the Terror would not be much felt so far from Paris. This prevision, based upon exact knowledge of the province, proved to be just. The Revolution did little devastation in Lower Normandy. Although, when Madame

41

de Dey visited her estates formerly, she used to see only the noble families of the province, she had from policy thrown her house open to the leading *bourgeois* of the town, and to the new authorities, striving to make them proud of their conquest of her, without arousing either hatred or jealousy in their minds. Gracious and amiable, endowed with that indescribable gentleness of manner which attracts without resort to self-abasement or to entreaties, she had succeeded in winning general esteem by the most exquisite tact, the wise promptings of which had enabled her to maintain her stand on the narrow line where she could satisfy the demands of that mixed society, without humiliating the self-esteem of the parvenus or offending that of her former friends.

About thirty-eight years of age, she still retained, not that fresh and buxom beauty which distinguishes the young women of Lower Normandy, but a slender and aristocratic beauty. Her features were small and refined, her figure slim and willowy. When she spoke, her pale face seemed to brighten and to take on life. Her great black eyes were full of suavity, but their placid, devout expression seemed to indicate that the active principle of her existence had ceased to be. Married in the flower of her youth to an old and jealous soldier, the falseness of her position in the centre of a dissipated court contributed much, no doubt, to cast a veil of serious melancholy over a face on which the charm and vivacity of love must formerly have shone bright.

Constantly obliged to restrain the ingenuous impulses of a woman, at a time when she still feels instead of reflecting, passion had remained unsullied in the depths of her heart. So it was that her principal attraction was due to the youthful simplicity which at intervals her face betrayed, and which gave to her ideas a naïve expression of desire. Her aspect imposed respect, but there were always in her bearing and in her voice symptoms of an outreaching towards an unknown future, as in a young girl; the most unsusceptible man soon found himself falling in love with her, and nevertheless retained a sort of respectful dread, inspired by her courteous manners, which were most impressive. Her soul, naturally great, and strengthened by painful struggles, seemed to be too far removed from the common herd, and men realised their limitations.

That soul necessarily demanded an exalted passion. So that Madame de Dey's affections were concentrated in a single sentiment, the sentiment of maternity. The happiness and pleasures of which her married life had been deprived, she found in her excessive love for her son. She loved him not only with the pure and profound devotion of a mother, but with the coquetry of a mistress, the jealousy of a wife. She was unhappy when separated from him, anxious during his absence, could never see enough of him, lived only in him and for him. In order to make men understand the strength of this feeling, it will suffice to add that this son was not only Madame de Dey's only child, but her last remaining relative, the only living being to whom she could attach the fears, the hopes, and the joys of her life. The late Count de Dey was the last scion of his family, as she was the last heiress of hers.

Thus human schemes and interests were in accord with the noblest cravings of the soul to intensify in the Countess's heart a sentiment which is always strong in women. She had brought up her son only with infinite difficulty, which had made him dearer than ever to her. Twenty times the doctors prophesied his death; but, trusting in her presentiments and her hopes, she had the inexpressible joy of seeing him pass through the dangers of childhood unscathed, and of exulting in the upbuilding of his constitution in spite of the decrees of the faculty.

Thanks to constant care, her son had grown and had attained such perfect development, that at twenty years of age he was considered one of the most accomplished cavaliers at Versailles. Lastly – a piece of good fortune which does not crown the efforts of all mothers – she was adored by her son; their hearts were bound together by sympathies that were fraternal. Even if they had not been connected by the decree of nature, they would have felt instinctively for each other that affection of one being for another so rarely met with in life. Appointed sub-lieutenant of dragoons at eighteen, the young man had complied with the prevailing ideas of the requirements of honour at that period by following the princes when they emigrated.

Thus Madame de Dey, of noble birth, wealthy, and the mother of an émigré, was fully alive to the dangers of her painful situation. As she had no other aim than to preserve a great fortune for her son, she had renounced the happiness of accompanying him; but, when she read the harsh laws by virtue of which the Republic daily confiscated the property of the émigrés at Carentan, she applauded herself for her courageous act. Was she not guarding her son's treasures at the peril of her life?

Then, when she learned of the shocking executions ordered by the Convention, she slept undisturbed, happy to know that her only treasure was in safety, far from all perils and all scaffolds. She took pleasure in the belief that she had adopted the best course to save all his fortunes at once. Making the concessions to this secret thought which the disasters of the time demanded, without compromising her womanly dignity or her aristocratic beliefs, she enveloped her sorrows in impenetrable mystery. She had realised the difficulties which awaited her at Carentan. To go thither and assume the first place in society – was it not equivalent to defying the scaffold every day? But, sustained by a mother's courage, she succeeded in winning the affection of the poor by relieving all sorts of misery indiscriminately, and made herself necessary to the rich by taking the lead in their pleasures.

She received the prosecuting attorney of the commune, the mayor, the president of the district, the public accuser, and even the judges of the Revolutionary Tribunal. The first four of these functionaries, being unmarried, paid court to her, in the hope of marrying her, whether by terrifying her by the injury which they had it in their power to do her, or by offering her protection. The public accuser, formerly an attorney at Caen, where he had been employed by the Countess, tried to win her love by conduct full of devotion and generosity. A dangerous scheme! He was the most formidable of all the suitors. He alone was thoroughly acquainted with the condition of his former client's large fortune. His passion was inevitably intensified by all the cravings of an avarice which rested upon almost unlimited power, upon the right of life or death throughout the district.

This man, who was still young, displayed so much nobility in his behaviour that Madame de Dey had been unable as yet to make up her mind concerning him. But, scorning the danger that lay in a contest of wits with Normans, she employed the inventive genius and the cunning which nature has allotted to woman, to play those rivals against one another. By gaining time, she hoped to arrive safe and sound at the end of her troubles. At that time, the royalists in the interior of France flattered themselves that each day would see the close of the Revolution; and that conviction was the ruin of a great many of them.

Despite these obstacles, the Countess had skilfully maintained her independence down to the day when, with incomprehensible imprudence, she had conceived the idea of closing her door. The interest which she inspired was so profound and so genuine that the people who came to her house that evening were greatly distressed when they learned that it was impossible for her to receive them. Then, with the outspoken curiosity which is a part of provincial manners, they inquired concerning the misfortune, the sorrow, or the disease which had afflicted Madame de Dey. To these questions, an old housekeeper called Brigitte replied that her mistress had shut herself into her room, and would not see anybody, not even her servants. The cloistral existence, so to speak, which the people of a small town lead, gives birth in them to such an unconquerable habit of analysing and commenting upon the actions of other people, that, after expressing their sympathy for Madame de Dey, without an idea whether she was really happy or unhappy, they all began to speculate upon the causes of her abrupt seclusion.

'If she were ill,' said one curious individual, 'she would have sent for the doctor; but the doctor was at my house all day, playing chess. He said with a laugh that in these days there is but one disease, and that is unfortunately incurable.

This jest was put forward apologetically. Thereupon, men, women, old men, and maidens began to search the vast field of conjecture. Every one fancied that he caught a glimpse of a secret, and that secret engrossed the imaginations of them all. The next day, the suspicions became embittered. As life in a small town is open to all, the women were the first to learn that Brigitte had laid in more supplies than usual at the market. That fact could not be denied. Brigitte had been seen in the morning, in the square, and – a most extraordinary thing – she had bought the only hare that was offered for sale. Now the whole town knew that Madame de Dey did not like game. The hare became the starting-point for endless suppositions. When taking their daily walk, old men observed in the Countess's house a sort of concentrated activity which was made manifest by the very precautions which the servants took to conceal it. The valet was seen beating a rug in the garden; on the day before, no one would have paid any heed to it; but that rug became a link in the chain of evidence to support the romances which everybody was engaged in constructing. Every person had his own.

On the second day, when they learned that Madame de Dey proclaimed that she was indisposed, the principal persons of Carentan met in the evening at the house of the Mayor's brother, an ex-merchant, a married man, of upright character and generally esteemed, and for whom the Countess entertained a high regard. There all the aspirants to the rich widow's hand had a more or less probable story to tell; and each of them hoped to turn to his advantage the secret circumstances which forced her to compromise herself thus. The public accuser imagined a complete drama in which Madame de Dey's son was brought to her house by night.

The mayor favoured the idea of a priest who had not taken the oath, arriving from La Vendée and asking her for shelter; but the purchase of a hare on Friday embarrassed the mayor greatly. The president of the district was strong in his conviction that it was a leader of Chouans or of Vendeans, hotly pursued. Others suggested a nobleman escaped from one of the prisons of Paris. In short, one and all suspected the Countess of being guilty of one of those acts of generosity which the laws of that day stigmatised as crimes, and which might lead to the scaffold. The public accuser said in an undertone that they must hold their tongues, and try to snatch the unfortunate woman from the abyss towards which she was rapidly precipitating herself.

'If you talk about this business,' he added, 'I shall be obliged to interfere, to search her house, and then —'

He did not finish his sentence, but they all understood his reticence.

The Countess's sincere friends were so alarmed for her that, during the morning of the third day, the procureur-syndic of the commune caused his wife to write her a note to urge her to receive as usual that evening. The old merchant, being bolder, called at Madame de Dey's house in the morning. Trusting in the service which he proposed to render her, he demanded to be shown to her presence, and was thunderstruck when he saw her in the garden, engaged in cutting the last flowers from the beds, to supply her vases.

'Doubtless she has been sheltering her lover,' said the old man to himself, seized with compassion for the fascinating woman.

The strange expression on the Countess's face confirmed him in his suspicions. Deeply touched by that devotion so natural to a woman, and which always moves our admiration, because all men are flattered by the sacrifices which a woman makes for a man, the merchant informed the Countess of the reports which were current in the town, and of the dangerous position in which she stood.

'But,' he said, as he concluded, 'although there are some among our officials who are not indisposed to forgive you for an act of heroism of which a priest is the object, no one will pity you if they discover that you are sacrificing yourself to the affections of the heart.'

At these words Madame de Dey looked at the old man with an expression of desperation and terror which made him shudder, old man though he was.

'Come,' said she, taking his hand and leading him to her bedroom, where, after making sure that they were alone, she took from her bosom a soiled and wrinkled letter. 'Read,' she cried, making a violent effort to pronounce the word.

She fell into her chair as if utterly overwhelmed. While the old gentleman was feeling for his spectacles and wiping them, she fastened her eyes upon him and scrutinised him for the first time with curiosity; then she said softly, in an altered voice:

'I trust you.'

'Am I not sharing your crime?' replied the old man, simply.

She started; for the first time her heart found itself in sympathy with another heart in that little town. The old merchant suddenly understood both the distress and the joy of the Countess. Her son had taken part in the Granville expedition; he wrote to his mother from prison, imparting to her one sad but sweet hope. Having no doubt of his success in escaping, he mentioned three days in which he might appear at her house in disguise. The fatal letter contained heartrending farewells in case he should not be at Carentan on the evening of the third day; and he begged his mother to hand a considerable sum of money to the messenger, who had undertaken to carry that letter to her through innumerable perils. The paper shook in the old man's hand.

'And this is the third day!' cried Madame de Dey, as she sprang to her feet, seized the letter, and began to pace the floor.

'You have been imprudent,' said the merchant; 'why did you lay in provisions?'

'Why, he may arrive almost starved, worn out with fatigue, and —'

She did not finish.

'I am sure of my brother,' said the old man, 'and I will go and enlist him on your side.'

In this emergency the old tradesman recovered the shrewdness which he had formerly displayed in his business, and gave advice instinct with prudence and sagacity. After agreeing upon all that they were both to say and to do, the old man went about, on cleverly devised pretexts, to the principal houses of Carentan, where he announced that Madame de Dey, whom he had just seen, would receive that evening in spite of her indisposition. Pitting his shrewdness against the inborn Norman cunning, in the examination to which each family subjected him in regard to the nature of the Countess's illness, he succeeded in leading astray almost everybody who was interested in that mysterious affair. His first visit produced a marvellous effect.

He stated, in the presence of a gouty old lady, that Madame de Dey had nearly died of an attack of gout in the stomach; as the famous Tronchin had once recommended her, in such a case, to place on her chest the skin of a hare, flayed alive, and to stay in bed and not move, the Countess, who had been at death's door two days before, having followed scrupulously

Tronchin's advice, found herself sufficiently recovered to see those who cared to call on her that evening. That fable had a prodigious success, and the Carentan doctor, a royalist in secret, added to its effect by the air of authority with which he discussed the remedy. Nevertheless, suspicion had taken too deep root in the minds of some obstinate persons, or some philosophers, to be entirely dispelled; so that, in the evening, those who were regular habitués of Madame de Dey's salon arrived there early; some in order to watch her face, others from friendly regard; and the majority were impressed by the marvellous nature of her recovery.

They found the Countess seated at the corner of the huge fireplace of her salon, which was almost as modestly furnished as those of the people of Carentan; for, in order not to offend the sensitive self-esteem of her guests, she denied herself the luxury to which she had always been accustomed, and had changed nothing in her house. The floor of the reception-room was not even polished. She left old-fashioned dark tapestries on the walls, she retained the native furniture, burned tallow candles, and followed the customs of the town, espousing provincial life, and recoiling neither from the most rasping pettinesses nor the most unpleasant privations. But, realising that her guests would forgive her for any display of splendour which aimed at their personal comfort, she neglected nothing when it was a question of affording them enjoyment; so that she always gave them excellent dinners. She even went so far as to make a pretence at miserliness, to please those calculating minds; and after causing certain concessions in the way of luxurious living to be extorted from her, she seemed to comply with a good grace.

About seven o'clock in the evening, therefore, the best of the uninteresting society of Carentan was assembled at her house, and formed a large circle about the fireplace. The mistress of the house, sustained in her misery by the compassionate glances which the old tradesman bestowed upon her, submitted with extraordinary courage to the minute questionings, the trivial and stupid reasoning of her guests. But at every blow of the knocker at her door, and whenever she heard footsteps in the street, she concealed her emotion by raising some question of interest to the welfare of the province. She started noisy discussions concerning the quality of the season's cider, and was so well seconded by her confidant that her company almost forgot to watch her, her manner was so natural and her self-possession so imperturbable. The public accuser and one of the judges of the Revolutionary Tribunal sat silent, carefully watching every movement of her face and listening to every sound in the house, notwithstanding the uproar; and on several occasions they asked her very embarrassing questions, which, however, the Countess answered with marvellous presence of mind. Mothers have such an inexhaustible store of courage! When Madame de Dey had arranged the card-tables, placed everybody at a table of boston, reversis, or whist, she remained a few moments talking with some young people, with the utmost nonchalance, playing her part like a consummate actress. She suggested a game of lotto – said that she alone knew where it was, and disappeared.

'I am suffocating, my poor Brigitte!' she cried, wiping away the tears that gushed from her eyes, which gleamed with fever, anxiety, and impatience. 'He does not come,' she continued, looking about the chamber to which she had flown. 'Here, I breathe again and I live. A few moments more, and he will be here; for he still lives, I am certain; my heart tells me so! Do you hear nothing, Brigitte? Oh! I would give the rest of my life to know whether he is in prison or travelling through the country! I would like not to think —'

She looked about again to make sure that everything was in order in the room. A bright fire was burning on the hearth; the shutters were carefully closed; the furniture glistened with cleanliness; the way in which the bed was made proved that the Countess had assisted Brigitte in the smallest details; and her hopes betrayed themselves in the scrupulous care which seemed to have been taken in that room, where the sweet charm of love and its most chaste caresses exhaled in the perfume of the flowers. A mother alone could have anticipated the desires of a soldier, and have arranged to fulfil them all so perfectly. A dainty meal, choice wines, clean linen, and dry shoes – in a word, all that was likely to be necessary or agreeable to a weary traveller was there set forth, so that he need lack nothing, so that the joy of home might make known to him a mother's love.

'Brigitte?' said the Countess in a heartrending tone, as she placed a chair at the table, as if to give reality to her longings, to intensify the strength of her illusions.

'Oh! he will come, madame; he isn't far away. I don't doubt that he's alive and on his way here,' replied Brigitte. 'I put a key in the Bible and I held it on my fingers while Cottin read the Gospel of St. John; and, madame, the key didn't turn.'

'Is that a sure sign?' asked the Countess.

'Oh! it is certain, madame; I would wager my salvation that he is still alive. God can't make a mistake.'

'Despite the danger that awaits him here, I would like right well to see him.'

'Poor Monsieur Auguste!' cried Brigitte; 'I suppose he is somewhere on the road, on foot!'

'And there is the church clock striking eight!' cried the Countess, in dismay.

She was afraid that she had remained longer than she ought in that room, where she had faith in the life of her son because she looked upon all that meant life to him. She went downstairs; but before entering the salon, she stood a moment in the vestibule, listening to see if any sound woke the silent echoes of the town. She smiled at Brigitte's husband, who was on sentry-duty, and whose eyes seemed dazed by dint of strained attention to the murmurs in the square and in the streets. She saw her son in everything and everywhere. In a moment she returned to the salon, affecting a jovial air, and began to play lotto with some young girls; but from time to time she complained of feeling ill, and returned to her chair at the fireplace.

Such was the condition of persons and things in the house of Madame de Dey, while, on the road from Paris to Cherbourg, a young man dressed in a dark carmagnole, the regulation costume at that period, strode along towards Carentan. At the beginning of the conscription, there was little or no discipline. The demands of the moment made it impossible for the Republic to equip all of its soldiers at once, and it was no rare thing to see the roads covered with conscripts still wearing their civilian dress. These young men marched in advance of their battalions to the halting-places, or loitered behind, for their progress was regulated by their ability to endure the fatigue of a long march.

The traveller with whom we have to do was some distance in advance of the column of conscripts on its way to Cherbourg, which the Mayor of Carentan was momentarily expecting, in order to distribute lodging-tickets among them. The young man walked with a heavy but still firm step, and his bearing seemed to indicate that he had long been familiar with the hardships of military life. Although the moon was shining on the pastures about Carentan, he had noticed some great white clouds which seemed on the point of discharging snow upon the country, and the fear of being surprised by a storm doubtless quickened his gait, which was more rapid than his weariness made comfortable. He had an almost empty knapsack on his back, and carried in his hand a boxwood cane, cut from one of the high, broad hedges formed by that shrub around most of the estates in Lower Normandy.

The solitary traveller entered Carentan, whose towers, of fantastic aspect in the moonlight, had appeared to him a moment before. His steps awoke the echoes of the silent streets, where he met no one; he was obliged to ask a weaver who was still at work to point out the Mayor's abode. That magistrate lived only a short distance away, and the conscript soon found himself safe under the porch of his house, where he seated himself on a stone bench, waiting for the lodging-ticket which he had asked for. But, being summoned by the Mayor, he appeared before him, and was subjected to a careful examination. The soldier was a young man of attractive appearance, who apparently belonged to some family of distinction. His manner indicated noble birth, and the intelligence due to a good education was manifest in his features.

'What is your name?' the Mayor asked, with a shrewd glance at him.

'Julien Jussieu,' replied the conscript.

'And you come from —?' said the magistrate, with an incredulous smile.

'From Paris.'

'Your comrades must be far behind?' continued the Norman in a mocking tone.

'I am three leagues ahead of the battalion.'

'Doubtless some sentimental reason brings you to Carentan, citizen conscript?' queried the Mayor, slyly. 'It is all right,' he added, imposing silence, with a wave of the hand, upon the young man, who was about to speak. 'We know where to send you. Here,' he said, handing him the lodging-ticket; 'here, *Citizen Jussieu.*'

There was a perceptible tinge of irony in the tone in which the magistrate uttered these last two words, as he held out a ticket upon which Madame de Dey's name was written. The young man read the address with an air of curiosity.

'He knows very well that he hasn't far to go, and when he gets outside, it won't take him long to cross the square,' cried the Mayor, speaking to himself, while the young man went out. 'He's a bold young fellow. May God protect him! He has an answer for everything. However, if any other than I had asked to see his papers, he would have been lost!'

At that moment the clock of Carentan struck half-past nine; the torches were being lighted in Madame de Dey's ante-room, and the servants were assisting their masters and mistresses to put on their cloaks, their overcoats, and their mantles; the card-players had settled their accounts and were about to withdraw in a body, according to the usual custom in all small towns.

'It seems that the public accuser proposes to remain,' said a lady, observing that the important functionary was missing when they were about to separate to seek their respective homes, after exhausting all the formulas of leave-taking.

The redoubtable magistrate was in fact alone with the Countess, who waited in fear and trembling until it should please him to go.

'Citizeness,' he said at length, after a long silence in which there was something horrible, 'I am here to see that the laws of the Republic are observed.'

Madame de Dey shuddered.

'Have you no revelations to make to me?' he demanded.

'None,' she replied in amazement.

'Ah, madame!' cried the accuser, sitting down beside her and changing his tone, 'at this moment, for lack of a word, either you or I may bring our heads to the scaffold. I have observed your temperament, your heart, your manners, too closely to share the error into which you have led your guests tonight. You are expecting your son, I am absolutely certain.'

The Countess made a gesture of denial; but she had turned pale, the muscles of her face had contracted, by virtue of the overpowering necessity to display a deceitful calmness, and the accuser's implacable eye lost none of her movements.

'Very well; receive him,' continued the revolutionary magistrate; 'but do not let him remain under your roof later than seven o'clock in the morning. At daybreak I shall come here armed with a denunciation which I shall procure.'

She gazed at him with a stupefied air, which would have aroused the pity of a tiger.

'I shall prove,' he said in a gentle tone, 'the falseness of the denunciation by a thorough search, and the nature of my report will place you out of the reach of any future suspicion. I shall speak of your patriotic gifts, of your true citizenship, and we shall *all* be saved.'

Madame de Dey feared a trap; she did not move, but her face was on fire and her tongue was frozen. A blow of the knocker rang through the house.

'Ah!' cried the terrified mother, falling on her knees. 'Save him! save him!'

'Yes, let us save him,' rejoined the public accuser, with a passionate glance at her; 'let us save him though it cost *us* our lives.'

'I am lost!' she cried, while the accuser courteously raised her.

'Oh madame!' he replied, with a grand oratorical gesture, 'I do not choose to owe you to any one but yourself.'

'Madame, here he —' cried Brigitte, who thought that her mistress was alone.

At sight of the public accuser, the old servant, whose face was flushed with joy, became rigid and deathly pale.

'What is it, Brigitte?' asked the magistrate, in a mild and meaning tone.

'A conscript that the Mayor has sent here to lodge,' replied the servant, showing the ticket.

'That is true,' said the accuser, after reading the paper; 'a battalion is to arrive here tonight.'

And he went out.

The Countess was too anxious at that moment to believe in the sincerity of her former attorney to entertain the slightest suspicion; she ran swiftly upstairs, having barely strength enough to stand upright; then she opened the door of her bedroom, saw her son, and rushed into his arms, well-nigh lifeless.

'O my son, my son!' she cried, sobbing, and covering him with frenzied kisses.

'Madame —' said the stranger.

'Oh! it isn't he!' she cried, stepping back in dismay and standing before the conscript, at whom she gazed with a haggard expression.

'Blessed Lord God, what a resemblance!' said Brigitte.

There was a moment's silence, and the stranger himself shuddered as the aspect of Madame de Dey.

'Ah, monsieur!' she said, leaning upon Brigitte's husband, and feeling then in all its force the grief of which the first pang had almost killed her; 'monsieur, I cannot endure to see you any longer; allow my servants to take my place and to attend to your wants.'

She went down to her own apartments, half carried by Brigitte and her old servant.

'What, madame!' cried the maid, 'is that man going to sleep in Monsieur Auguste's bed, wear Monsieur Auguste's slippers, eat the pie that I made for Monsieur Auguste? They may guillotine me, but I —'

'Brigitte!' cried Madame de Dey.

'Hold your tongue, chatterbox!' said her husband in a low voice; 'do you want to kill madame?'

At that moment the conscript made a noise in his room, drawing his chair to the table.

'I will not stay here,' cried Madame de Dey; 'I will go to the greenhouse, where I can hear better what goes on outside during the night.'

She was still wavering between fear of having lost her son and the hope of seeing him appear. The night was disquietingly silent. There was one ghastly moment for the

Countess, when the battalion of conscripts marched into town, and each man repaired to his lodging. There were disappointed hopes at every footstep and every sound; then nature resumed its terrible tranquillity. Towards morning the Countess was obliged to return to her room. Brigitte, who watched her mistress every moment, finding that she did not come out again, went to her room and found the Countess dead.

'She probably heard the conscript dressing and walking about in Monsieur Auguste's room, singing their cursed *Marseillaise* as if he were in a stable!' cried Brigitte. 'It was that which killed her!'

The Countess's death was caused by a more intense emotion, and probably by some terrible vision. At the precise moment when Madame de Dey died at Carentan, her son was shot in Le Morbihan. We might add this tragic story to the mass of other observations on that sympathy which defies the law of space – documents which some few solitary scholars are collecting with scientific curiosity, and which will one day serve as basis for a new science, a science which till now has lacked only its man of genius.

LA GRANDE BRETÈCHE

LA GRANDE BRETÈCHE

About one hundred yards from Vendôme, on the banks of the Loire, there stands an old dark-coloured house, surmounted by a very high roof, and so completely isolated that there is not in the neighbourhood a single evil-smelling tannery or wretched inn, such as we see on the outskirts of almost every small town. In front of the house is a small garden bordering the river, in which the boxwood borders of the paths, once neatly trimmed, now grow at their pleasure. A few willows, born in the Loire, have grown as rapidly as the hedge which encloses the garden, and half conceal the house. The plants which we call weeds adorn the slope of the bank with their luxuriant vegetation. The fruit-trees, neglected for ten years, bear no fruit; their offshoots form a dense undergrowth. The espaliers resemble hornbeam hedges. The paths, formerly gravelled, are overrun with purslane; but, to tell the truth, there are no well-marked paths. From the top of the mountain upon which hang the ruins of the old château of the Dukes of Vendôme, the only spot from which the eye can look into this enclosure, you would say to yourself that, at a period which it is difficult to determine, that little nook was the delight of some gentleman devoted to roses and tulips, to horticulture in short, but especially fond of fine fruit. You espy an arbour, or rather the ruins of an arbour, beneath which a table still stands, not yet entirely consumed by time. At sight of that garden, which is no longer a garden, one may divine the negative delights of the peaceful life which provincials lead, as one divines the existence of a worthy tradesman by reading the epitaph on his tombstone. To round out the melancholy yet soothing thoughts which fill the mind, there is on one of the walls a sun-dial, embellished with this commonplace Christian inscription: ULTIMAM COGITA. The roof of the house is terribly dilapidated, the blinds are always drawn, the balconies are covered with swallows' nests, the doors are

never opened. Tall weeds mark with green lines the cracks in
the steps; the ironwork is covered with rust. Moon, sun,
winter, summer, snow, have rotted the wood, warped the
boards, and corroded the paint.

The deathly silence which reigns there is disturbed only by
the birds, the cats, the martens, the rats and the mice, which
are at liberty to run about, to fight, and to eat one another at
their will. An invisible hand has written everywhere the word
MYSTERY. If, impelled by curiosity, you should go to inspect
the house on the street side, you would see a high gate, arched
at the top, in which the children of the neighbourhood have
made numberless holes. I learned later that that gate had been
condemned ten years before. Through these irregular breaches
you would be able to observe the perfect harmony between
the garden front and the courtyard front. The same disorder
reigns supreme in both. Tufts of weeds surround the pave-
ments. Enormous cracks furrow the walls, whose blackened
tops are enlaced by the countless tendrils of climbing plants.
The steps are wrenched apart, the bell-rope is rotten, the
gutters are broken. 'What fire from heaven has passed this
way? What tribunal has ordered salt to be strewn upon this
dwelling? Has God been insulted here? Has France been
betrayed?' Such are the questions which one asks one's self.
The reptiles crawl hither and thither without answering. That
empty and deserted house is an immense riddle, the solution
of which is known to no one.

It was formerly a small feudal estate and bore the name of La
Grande Bretèche. During my stay at Vendôme, where
Desplein had left me to attend a rich patient, the aspect of that
strange building became one of my keenest pleasures. Was it
not more than a mere ruin? Some souvenirs of undeniable
authenticity are always connected with a ruin; but that abode,
still standing, although in process of gradual demolition by an
avenging hand, concealed a secret, an unknown thought; at
the very least, it betrayed a caprice. More than once, in the
evening, I wandered in the direction of the hedge, now wild
and uncared for, which surrounded that enclosure. I defied
scratches, and made my way into that ownerless garden, that
estate which was neither public nor private; and I remained
whole hours there contemplating its disarray. Not even to

learn the story which would doubtless account for that
extraordinary spectacle, would I have asked a single question
of any Vendômese gossip. Straying about there, I composed
delightful romances, I abandoned myself to little orgies of
melancholy which enchanted me.

If I had learned the cause of that perhaps most commonplace
neglect, I should have lost the unspoken poesy with which I
intoxicated myself. To me that spot represented the most
diverse images of human life darkened by its misfortunes; now
it was the air of the cloister, minus the monks; again, the
perfect peace of the cemetery, minus the dead speaking their
epitaphic language; today, the house of the leper; tomorrow,
that of the Fates; but it was, above all, the image of the
province, with its meditation, with its hour-glass life. I have
often wept there, but never laughed. More than once I have
felt an involuntary terror, as I heard above my head the low
rustling made by the wings of some hurrying dove. The
ground is damp; you must beware of lizards, snakes, and
toads, which wander about there with the fearless liberty of
nature; above all, you must not fear the cold, for, after a few
seconds, you feel an icy cloak resting upon your shoulders like
the hand of the Commendator on the neck of Don Juan. One
evening I had shuddered there; the wind had twisted an old
rusty weather-vane, whose shrieks resembled a groan uttered
by the house at the moment that I was finishing a rather dismal
melodrama, by which I sought to explain to myself that
species of monumental grief. I returned to my inn, beset by
sombre thoughts. When I had supped, my hostess entered my
room with a mysterious air, and said to me:

'Here is Monsieur Regnault, monsieur.'

'Who is Monsieur Regnault?'

'What! monsieur doesn't know Monsieur Regnault? That's
funny!' she said, as she left the room.

Suddenly I saw a tall slender man, dressed in black, with his
hat in his hand, who entered the room like a ram ready to rush
at his rival, disclosing a retreating forehead, a small pointed
head, and a pale face, not unlike a glass of dirty water. You
would have said that he was the doorkeeper of some minister.
He wore an old coat, threadbare at the seams; but he had a
diamond in his shirt-frill and gold rings in his ears.

'To whom have I the honour of speaking, monsieur?' I asked him.

He took a chair, seated himself in front of my fire, placed his hat on my table, and replied, rubbing his hands:

'Ah! it's very cold! I am Monsieur Regnault, monsieur.'

I bowed, saying to myself:

'*Il Bondocani!* Look for him!'

'I am the notary at Vendôme,' he continued.

'I am delighted to hear it, monsieur,' I exclaimed, 'but I am not ready to make my will, for reasons best known to myself.'

'Just a minute,' he rejoined, raising his hand as if to impose silence upon me. 'I beg pardon, monsieur, I beg pardon! I have heard that you go to walk sometimes in the garden of La Grande Bretèche.'

'Yes, monsieur!'

'Just a minute,' he said, repeating his gesture; 'that practice constitutes a downright trespass. I have come, monsieur, in the name and as executor of the late Madame Comtesse de Merret, to beg you to discontinue your visits. Just a minute! I'm not a Turk, and I don't propose to charge you with a crime. Besides, it may well be that you are not aware of the circumstances which compel me to allow the finest mansion in Vendôme to fall to ruin. However, monsieur, you seem to be a man of education, and you must know that the law forbids entrance upon an enclosed estate under severe penalties. A hedge is as good as a wall. But the present condition of the house may serve as an excuse for your curiosity. I would ask nothing better than to allow you to go and come as you please in that house; but, as it is my duty to carry out the will of the testatrix, I have the honour, monsieur, to request you not to go into that garden again. Even I myself, monsieur, since the opening of the will, have never set foot inside that house, which, as I have had the honour to tell you, is a part of the estate of Madame de Merret. We simply reported the number of doors and windows, in order to fix the amount of the impost which I pay annually from the fund set aside for that purpose by the late countess. Ah! her will made a great deal of talk in Vendôme, monsieur.'

At that, he stopped to blow his nose, the excellent man. I respected his loquacity, understanding perfectly that the

administration of Madame de Merret's property was the
important event of his life – his reputation, his glory, his
Restoration. I must needs bid adieu to my pleasant reveries, to
my romances; so that I was not inclined to scorn the pleasure
of learning the truth from an official source.

'Would it be indiscreet, monsieur,' I asked him, 'to ask you
the reason of this extraordinary state of affairs?'

At that question an expression which betrayed all the
pleasure that a man feels who is accustomed to ride a hobby
passed over the notary's face. He pulled up his shirt collar with
a self-satisfied air, produced his snuff-box, opened it, offered
it to me, and at my refusal, took a famous pinch himself. He
was happy; the man who has no hobby has no idea of the
satisfaction that can be derived from life. A hobby is the
precise mean between passion and monomania. At that
moment I understood the witty expression of Sterne in all its
extent, and I had a perfect conception of the joy with which
Uncle Toby, with Trim's assistance, bestrode his battle-horse.

'Monsieur,' said Monsieur Regnault, 'I was chief clerk to
Master Roguin of Paris. An excellent office, of which you
may have heard? No? Why, it was made famous by a
disastrous failure. Not having sufficient money to practise in
Paris, at the price to which offices had risen in 1816, I came
here and bought the office of my predecessor. I had relatives in
Vendôme, among others a very rich aunt, who gave me her
daughter in marriage. Monsieur,' he continued after a brief
pause, 'three months after being licensed by the Keeper of the
Seals I was sent for one evening, just as I was going to bed (I
was not then married), by Madame Comtesse de Merret, to
come to her Château de Merret. Her maid, an excellent girl
who works in this inn today, was at my door with madame
comtesse's carriage. But, just a minute! I must tell you,
monsieur, that Monsieur Comte de Merret had gone to Paris
to die, two months before I came here. He died miserably
there, abandoning himself to excesses of all sorts. You
understand? – On the day of his departure madame comtesse
had left La Grande Bretèche and had dismantled it. Indeed,
some people declare that she burned the furniture and hang-
ings, and all chattels whatsoever now contained in the estate
leased by the said — What on earth am I saying? I beg pardon,

I thought I was dictating a lease. – That she burned them,' he continued, 'in the fields at Merret. Have you been to Merret, monsieur? No?' he said, answering his own question. 'Ah! that is a lovely spot! For about three months,' he continued, after a slight shake of the head, 'monsieur comte and madame comtesse led a strange life.

'They received no guests; madame lived on the ground floor, and monsieur on the first floor. When madame comtesse was left alone, she never appeared except at church. Later, in her own house, at her château, she refused to see the friends who came to see her. She was already much changed when she left La Grande Bretèche to go to Merret. The dear woman – I say "dear," because this diamond came from her; but I actually only saw her once – the excellent lady, then, was very ill; she had doubtless despaired of her health, for she died without calling a doctor; so that many of our ladies thought that she was not in full possession of her wits. My curiosity was therefore strangely aroused, monsieur, when I learned that Madame de Merret needed my services. I was not the only one who took an interest in that story. That same evening, although it was late, the whole town knew that I had gone to Merret. The maid answered rather vaguely the questions that I asked her on the road; she told me, however, that her mistress had received the sacrament from the curé of Merret during the day, and that she did not seem likely to live through the night.

'I reached the château about eleven o'clock; I mounted the main staircase. After passing through divers large rooms, high and dark, and as cold and damp as the devil, I reached the state bedchamber where the countess was. According to the reports that were current concerning that lady – I should never end, monsieur, if I should repeat all the stories that are told about her – I had thought of her as a coquette. But, if you please, I had much difficulty in finding her in the huge bed in which she lay. To be sure, to light that enormous wainscoted chamber of the old *régime*, where everything was so covered with dust that it made one sneeze simply to look at it, she had only one of those old-fashioned Argand lamps. Ah! but you have never been to Merret. Well, monsieur, the bed is one of those beds of the olden time, with a high canopy of flowered material. A small night-table stood beside the bed, and I saw upon it a copy of the *Imitation of Jesus Christ*, which, by the by, I bought for my wife, as well as the lamp. There was also a large couch for the attendant, and two chairs. Not a spark of fire. That was all the furniture. It wouldn't have filled ten lines in an inventory.

'Oh! my dear monsieur, if you had seen, as I then saw it, that huge room hung with dark tapestry, you would have imagined yourself transported into a genuine scene from a novel. It was icy cold; and, more than that, absolutely funereal,' he added, raising his arm with a theatrical gesture and pausing for a moment. 'By looking hard and walking close to the bed, I succeeded in discovering Madame de Merret, thanks to the lamp, the light of which shone upon the pillow. Her face was as yellow as wax, and resembled two clasped hands. She wore a lace cap, which revealed her lovely hair, as white as snow. She was sitting up, and seemed to retain that position with much difficulty. Her great black eyes, dulled by fever no doubt, and already almost lifeless, hardly moved beneath the bones which the eyebrows cover – these,' he said, pointing to the arch over his eyes. – 'Her brow was moist. Her fleshless hands resembled bones covered with tightly-drawn skin; her veins and muscles could be seen perfectly. She must have been very beautiful; but at that moment I was seized with an indefinable feeling at her aspect. Never before, according to those who laid her out, had a living creature attained such thinness without dying. In short, she was horrible to look at; disease had so wasted that woman that she was nothing more than a phantom. Her pale violet lips seemed not to move when she spoke to me. Although my profession had familiarised me with such spectacles, by taking me sometimes to the pillows of dying persons to take down their last wishes, I confess that the families in tears and despair whom I had seen were as nothing beside that solitary, silent woman in that enormous château.

'I did not hear the slightest sound, I could not detect the movement which the breathing of the sick woman should have imparted to the sheets that covered her; and I stood quite still, gazing at her in a sort of stupor. It seems to me that I am there now. At last her great eyes moved, she tried to raise her right hand, which fell back upon the bed, and these words

came from her mouth like a breath, for her voice had already
ceased to be a voice: "I have been awaiting you with much
impatience." – Her cheeks suddenly flushed. It was a great
effort for her to speak, monsieur. – "Madame," I said. She
motioned to me to be silent. At that moment the old nurse
rose and whispered in my ear: "Don't speak; madame comtesse
cannot bear to hear the slightest sound, and what you said
might excite her." – I sat down. A few moments later,
Madame de Merret collected all her remaining strength, to
move her right arm and thrust it, not without infinite
difficulty, beneath her bolster; she paused for just a moment;
then she made a last effort to withdraw her hand, and when
she finally produced a sealed paper, drops of sweat fell from
her brow. – "I place my will in your hands," she said. "Oh, *mon
Dieu!* oh!" – That was all. She grasped a crucifix that lay on
her bed, hastily put it to her lips, and died. The expression of
her staring eyes makes me shudder even now, when I think of
it. She must have suffered terribly! There was a gleam of joy in
her last glance, a sentiment which remained in her dead eyes.

'I carried the will away; and when it was opened, I found
that Madame de Merret had appointed me her executor. She
left all her property to the hospital at Vendôme with the
exception of a few individual legacies. But these were her
provisions with respect to La Grande Bretèche: she directed
me to leave her house, for fifty years from the day of her
death, in the same condition as at the moment that she died;
forbidding any person whatsoever to enter the rooms, forbidding the slightest repairs to be made, and even setting aside
a sum in order to hire keepers, if it should be found necessary,
to assure the literal execution of her purpose. At the expiration
of that period, if the desire of the testatrix has been carried out,
the house is to belong to my heirs, for monsieur knows that
notaries cannot accept legacies. If not, La Grande Bretèche is
to revert to whoever is entitled to it, but with the obligation to
comply with the conditions set forth in a codicil attached to
the will, which is not to be opened until the expiration of the
said fifty years. The will was not attacked; and so —'

At that, without finishing his sentence, the elongated notary
glanced at me with a triumphant air, and I made him
altogether happy by addressing a few compliments to him.

'Monsieur,' I said, 'you have made a profound impression upon me, so that I think I see that dying woman, paler than her sheets; her gleaming eyes terrify me; and I shall dream of her tonight. But you must have formed some conjecture concerning the provision of that extraordinary will.'

'Monsieur,' he said with a comical reserve, 'I never allow myself to judge the conduct of those persons who honour me by giving me a diamond.'

I soon loosened the tongue of the scrupulous Vendômese notary, who communicated to me, not without long digressions, observations due to the profound politicians of both sexes whose decrees are law in Vendôme. But those observations were so contradictory and so diffuse that I almost fell asleep, despite the interest I took in that authentic narrative. The dull and monotonous tone of the notary, who was accustomed, no doubt, to listen to himself, and to force his clients and his fellow citizens to listen to him, triumphed over my curiosity.

'Aha! many people, monsieur,' he said to me on the landing, 'would like to live forty-five years more; but just a minute!' and with a sly expression, he placed his right forefinger on his nose, as if he would have said: 'Just mark what I say.' – 'But to do that, to do that,' he added, 'a man must be less than sixty.'

I closed my door, having been roused from my apathy by this last shaft, which the notary considered very clever; then I seated myself in my easy-chair, placing my feet on the andirons. I was soon absorbed in an imaginary romance à la Radcliffe, based upon the judicial observations of Monsieur Regnault, when my door, under the skilful manipulation of a woman's hand, turned upon its hinges. My hostess appeared, a stout red-faced woman, of excellent disposition, who had missed her vocation: she was a Fleming, who should have been born in a picture by Teniers.

'Well, monsieur,' she said, 'no doubt Monsieur Regnault has given you his story of La Grande Bretèche?'

'Yes, Madame Lepas.'

'What did he tell you?'

I repeated in a few words the chilling and gloomy story of Madame de Merret. At each sentence my hostess thrust out

her neck, gazing at me with the true innkeeper's perspicacity –
a sort of happy medium between the instinct of the detective,
the cunning of the spy, and the craft of the trader.

'My dear Madame Lepas,' I added, as I concluded, 'you
evidently know more, eh? If not, why should you have come
up here?'

'Oh! on an honest woman's word, as true as my name's
Lepas —'

'Don't swear; your eyes are big with a secret. You knew
Monsieur de Merret. What sort of man was he?'

'Bless my soul! Monsieur de Merret was a fine man, whom
you never could see the whole of, he was so long; an excellent
gentleman, who came here from Picardy, and who had his
brains very near his cap, as we say here. He paid cash for
everything, in order not to have trouble with anybody. You
see, he was lively. We women all found him very agreeable.'

'Because he was lively?' I asked.

'That may be,' she said. 'You know, monsieur, that a man
must have had something in front of him, as they say, to
marry Madame de Merret, who, without saying anything
against the others, was the loveliest and richest woman in the
whole province. She had about twenty thousand francs a year.
The whole town went to her wedding. The bride was dainty
and attractive, a real jewel of a woman. Ah! they made a
handsome couple at that time!'

'Did they live happily together?'

'Oh, dear! oh, dear! yes and no, so far as any one could tell;
for, as you can imagine, we folks didn't live on intimate terms
with them. Madame de Merret was a kind-hearted woman,
very pleasant, who had to suffer sometimes perhaps from her
husband's quick temper; but although he was a bit proud, we
liked him. You see, it was his business to be like that; when a
man is noble, you know —'

'However, some catastrophe must have happened, to make
Monsieur and Madame de Merret separate so violently?'

'I didn't say there was any catastrophe, monsieur. I don't
know anything about it.'

'Good! I am sure now that you know all about it.'

'Well, monsieur, I will tell you all I know. When I saw
Monsieur Regnault come up to your room, I had an idea that

he would talk to you about Madame de Merret in connection with La Grande Bretèche. That gave me the idea of consulting with monsieur, who seems to me a man of good judgment and incapable of playing false with a poor woman like me, who never did anybody any harm, and yet who's troubled by her conscience. Up to this time I've never dared to speak out to the people of this neighbourhood, for they're all sharp-tongued gossips. And then, monsieur, I've never had a guest stay in my inn so long as you have, and to whom I could tell the story of the fifteen thousand francs.'

'My dear Madame Lepas,' I said, arresting the flood of her words, 'if your confidence is likely to compromise me, I wouldn't be burdened with it for a moment, for anything in the world.'

'Don't be afraid,' she said, interrupting me; 'you shall see.'

This eagerness on her part made me think that I was not the only one to whom my worthy hostess had communicated the secret of which I dreaded to be the only confidant, and I listened.

'Monsieur,' she began, 'when the Emperor sent Spanish or other prisoners of war here, I had to board, at the expense of the government, a young Spaniard who was sent to Vendôme on parole. In spite of the parole, he went every day to show himself to the subprefect. He was a Spanish grandee! Nothing less! He had a name ending in *os* and *dia*, something like Bagos de Férédia. I have his name written on my register; you can read it if you wish. He was a fine young man for a Spaniard, who they say are all ugly. He was only five feet two or three inches tall, but he was well-built; he had little hands, which he took care of – oh! you should have seen; he had as many brushes for his hands as a woman has for all purposes! He had long black hair, a flashing eye, and rather a copper-coloured skin, which I liked all the same. He wore such fine linen as I never saw before on any one, although I have entertained princesses, and among others General Bertrand, the Duke and Duchess d'Abrantès, Monsieur Decazes, and the King of Spain. He didn't eat much; but he had polite and pleasant manners, so that I couldn't be angry with him for it. Oh! I was very fond of him, although he didn't say four words a day, and it was impossible to have the slightest conversation with him; if any one spoke to him, he wouldn't answer; it was a fad, a mania that they all have, so they tell me. He read his breviary like a priest, he went to mass and to the services regularly. Where did he sit? We noticed that later: about two steps from Madame de Merret's private chapel. As he took his seat there the first time that he came to the church, nobody imagined that there was any design in it. Besides, he never took his face off his prayer-book, the poor young man! In the evening, monsieur, he used to walk on the mountain, among the ruins of the château. That was the poor man's only amusement; he was reminded of his own country there. They say that there's nothing but mountains in Spain.

'Very soon after he came here he began to stay out late. I was anxious when he didn't come home till midnight; but we all got used to his whim; he would take the key of the door, and we wouldn't wait for him. He lived in a house that we have on Rue de Casernes. Then one of our stablemen told us that one night, when he took the horses to drink, he thought he saw the Spanish grandee swimming far out in the river, like a real fish. When he came back, I told him to be careful of the eel-grass; he seemed vexed that he had been seen in the water. At last, monsieur, one day, or rather one morning, we didn't find him in his room; he hadn't come home. By hunting carefully everywhere, I found a note in his table drawer, where there were fifty of the Spanish gold-pieces which they call *portugaises*, and which were worth about five thousand francs; and then there were ten thousand francs' worth of diamonds in a little sealed box. His note said that in case he didn't return, he left us this money and his diamonds, on condition that we would found masses to thank God for his escape and his salvation. In those days I still had my man, who went out to look for him. And here's the funny part of the story: he brought back the Spaniard's clothes, which he found under a big stone in a sort of a shed by the river, on the château side, almost opposite La Grande Bretèche.

'My husband went there so early that no one saw him; he burned the clothes after reading the letter, and we declared, according to Count Férédia's wish, that he had escaped. The subprefect set all the gendarmerie on his track, but, bless my soul! they never caught him. Lepas believed that the Spaniard had drowned himself. For my part, monsieur, I don't think it; I think rather that he was mixed up in Madame de Merret's business, seeing that Rosalie told me that the crucifix that her mistress thought so much of that she had it buried with her, was made of ebony and silver; now, in the early part of his stay here, Monsieur Férédia had one of silver and ebony, which I didn't see afterwards. Tell me now, monsieur, isn't it true that I needn't have any remorse about the Spaniard's fifteen thousand francs, and that they are fairly mine?'

'Certainly. But did you never try to question Rosalie?' I asked her.

'Oh! yes, indeed, monsieur. But would you believe it? That girl is like a wall. She knows something, but it's impossible to make her talk.'

After conversing a moment more with me, my hostess left me beset by undefined and dismal thoughts, by a romantic sort of curiosity, a religious terror not unlike the intense emotion that seizes us when we enter a dark church at night and see a dim light in the distance under the lofty arches; a vague figure gliding along, or the rustling of a dress or a surplice; it makes us shudder. La Grande Bretèche and its tall weeds, its condemned windows, its rusty ironwork, its closed doors, its deserted rooms, suddenly appeared before me in fantastic guise. I tried to penetrate that mysterious abode, seeking there the kernel of that sombre story, of that drama which had caused the death of three persons. In my eyes Rosalie was the most interesting person in Vendôme. As I scrutinised her, I detected traces of some inmost thought, despite the robust health that shone upon her plump cheeks. There was in her some seed of remorse or of hope; her manner announced a secret, as does that of the devotee who prays with excessive fervour, or that of the infanticide, who constantly hears her child's last cry. However, her attitude was artless and natural, her stupid smile had no trace of criminality, and you would have voted her innocent simply by glancing at the large handkerchief with red and blue squares which covered her vigorous bust, confined by a gown with white and violet stripes.

'No,' I thought, 'I won't leave Vendôme without learning the whole story of La Grande Bretèche. To obtain my end, I will become Rosalie's friend, if it is absolutely necessary.'

'Rosalie?' I said one evening.

'What is it, monsieur?'

'You are not married?'

She started slightly.

'Oh! I sha'n't lack men when I take a fancy to be unhappy!' she said, with a laugh.

She speedily overcame her inward emotion; for all women, from the great lady down to the servant at the inn, have a self-possession which is peculiar to them.

'You are fresh and appetising enough not to lack suitors. But tell me, Rosalie, why did you go to work in an inn when you left Madame de Merret's? Didn't she leave you some money?'

'Oh, yes! but my place is the best in Vendôme, monsieur.'

This reply was one of those which judges and lawyers call dilatory. Rosalie seemed to me to occupy in that romantic story the position of the square in the middle of the chessboard; she was at the very centre of interest and of truth; she seemed to me to be tied up in the clue; there was in that girl the last chapter of a romance; and so, from that moment, Rosalie became the object of my attentions. By dint of studying the girl, I observed in her, as in all women to whom we devote all our thoughts, a multitude of good qualities: she was neat and clean, and she was fine-looking – that goes without saying; she had also all the attractions which our desire imparts to women, in whatever station of life they may be. A fortnight after the notary's visit, I said to Rosalie one evening, or rather one morning, for it was very early:

'Tell me all that you know about Madame de Merret.'

'Oh, don't ask me that, Monsieur Horace!' she replied in alarm.

Her pretty face darkened, her bright colour vanished, and her eyes lost their humid, innocent light. But I insisted.

'Well,' she rejoined, 'as you insist upon it, I will tell you; but keep my secret.'

'Of course, of course, my dear girl; I will keep all your secrets with the probity of a thief, and that is the most loyal probity that exists.'

'If it's all the same to you,' she said, 'I prefer that it should be with your own.'

Thereupon she arranged her neckerchief, and assumed the attitude of a story-teller; for there certainly is an attitude of trust and security essential to the telling of a story. The best stories are told at a certain hour, and at the table, as we all are now. No one ever told a story well while standing, or fasting. But if it were necessary to reproduce faithfully Rosalie's diffuse eloquence, a whole volume would hardly suffice. Now, as the event of which she gave me a confused account occupied, between the loquacity of the notary and that of Madame Lepas, the exact position of the mean terms of an arithmetical proportion between the two extremes, it is only necessary for me to repeat it to you in a few words. Therefore I abridge.

The room which Madame de Merret occupied at La Grande Bretèche was on the ground floor. A small closet, about four feet deep, in the wall, served as her wardrobe. Three months before the evening, the incidents of which I am about to narrate, Madame de Merret had been so seriously indisposed that her husband left her alone in her room and slept in a room on the first floor. By one of those chances which it is impossible to foresee, he returned home, on the evening in question, two hours later than usual, from the club to which he was accustomed to go to read the newspapers and to talk politics with the people of the neighbourhood. His wife supposed that he had come home, and had gone to bed and to sleep. But the invasion of France had given rise to a lively discussion; the game of billiards had been very close, and he had lost forty francs, an enormous sum at Vendôme, where everybody hoards money, and where manners are confined within the limits of a modesty worthy of all praise, which perhaps is the source of the true happiness of which no Parisian has a suspicion.

For some time past Monsieur de Merret had contented himself with asking Rosalie if his wife were in bed; at the girl's reply, always in the affirmative, he went immediately to his own room with the readiness born of habit and confidence. But on returning home that evening, he took it into his head to go to Madame de Merret's room, to tell her of his misadventure and perhaps also to console himself for it. During dinner he had remarked that Madame de Merret was

very coquettishly dressed; he said to himself as he walked
home from the club, that his wife was no longer ill, that her
convalescence had improved her; but he perceived it, as
husbands notice everything, a little late. Instead of calling
Rosalie, who at that moment was busy in the kitchen,
watching the cook and the coachman play a difficult hand of
brisque, Monsieur de Merret went to his wife's room, lighted
by his lantern, which he had placed on the top step of the
stairs. His footstep, easily recognised, resounded under the
arches of the corridor. At that instant that he turned the knob
of his wife's door, he fancied that he heard the door of the
closet that I have mentioned close; but when he entered,
Madame de Merret was alone, standing in front of the hearth.
The husband naïvely concluded that Rosalie was in the closet;
however, a suspicion, that rang in his ears like the striking of a
clock, made him distrustful; he looked at his wife and detected
in her eyes something indefinable of confusion and dismay.

'You come home very late,' she said.

That voice, usually so pure and so gracious, seemed to him
slightly changed. He made no reply, but at that moment
Rosalie entered the room. That was a thunderclap to him. He
walked about the room, from one window to another, with a
uniform step and with folded arms.

'Have you learned anything distressing, or are you ill?' his
wife timidly asked him, while Rosalie undressed her.

He made no reply.

'You may go,' said Madame de Merret to her maid; 'I will
put on my curl-papers myself.'

She divined some catastrophe simply from the expression of
her husband's face, and she preferred to be alone with him.
When Rosalie was gone, or was supposed to be gone, for she
stayed for some moments in the corridor, Monsieur de Merret
took his stand in front of his wife, and said to her coldly:

'Madame, there is someone in your closet?'

She looked at her husband calmly, and replied simply:

'No, monsieur.'

That 'no' tore Monsieur de Merret's heart, for he did not
believe it; and yet his wife had never seemed to him purer and
more holy than she seemed at that moment. He rose to open
the closet door; Madame de Merret took his hand, stopped

him, looked at him with a melancholy expression, and said in a voice strangely moved:

'If you find no one, reflect that all is at an end between us!'

The indescribable dignity of his wife's attitude reawoke the gentleman's profound esteem for her, and inspired in him one of those resolutions which require only a vaster theatre in order to become immortal.

'No,' he said, 'I will not do it, Josephine. In either case, we should be separated for ever. Listen; I know all the purity of your soul, and I know that you lead the life of a saint, and that you would not commit a mortal sin to save your life.'

At these words, Madame de Merret looked at her husband with haggard eye.

'See, here is your crucifix; swear to me before God that there is no one there, and I will believe you, I will never open that door.'

Madame de Merret took the crucifix and said:

'I swear it.'

'Louder,' said the husband, 'and repeat after me: "I swear before God that there is no one in that closet."'

She repeated the words without confusion.

'It is well,' said Monsieur de Merret coldly. After a moment's silence: 'This is a very beautiful thing that I did not know you possessed,' he said, as he examined the crucifix of ebony encrusted with silver and beautifully carved.

'I found it at Duvivier's; when that party of prisoners passed through Vendôme last year, he bought it off a Spanish monk.'

'Ah!' said Monsieur de Merret, replacing the crucifix on the nail. And he rang. Rosalie did not keep him waiting. Monsieur de Merret walked hastily to meet her, led her into the embrasure of the window looking over the garden, and said to her in a low voice:

'I know that Gorenflot wants to marry you, that poverty alone prevents you from coming together, and that you have told him that you would not be his wife until he found some way to become a master mason. Well, go to him, and tell him to come here with his trowel and his tools. Manage so as not to wake anybody in his house but him; his fortune will exceed your desires. Above all, go out of this house without chattering, or —'

He frowned. Rosalie started, and he called her back.

'Here, take my pass-key,' he said.

'Jean!' shouted Monsieur de Merret in the corridor, in a voice of thunder.

Jean, who was both his coachman and his confidential man, left his game of *brisque* and answered the summons.

'Go to bed, all of you,' said his master, motioning to him to come near. And he added, but in an undertone: 'When they are all asleep, *asleep*, do you understand, you will come down and let me know.'

Monsieur de Merret, who had not lost sight of his wife while giving his orders, calmly returned to her side in front of the fire, and began to tell her about the game of billiards and the discussion at the club. When Rosalie returned she found monsieur and madame talking most amicably. The gentleman had recently had plastered all the rooms which composed his reception-apartment on the ground floor. Plaster is very scarce in Vendôme, and the cost of transportation increases the price materially; so he had purchased quite a large quantity, knowing that he would readily find customers for any that he might have left. That circumstance suggested the design which he proceeded to carry out.

'Gorenflot is here, monsieur,' said Rosalie in an undertone.

'Let him come in,' replied the Picard gentleman aloud.

Madame de Merret turned pale when she saw the mason.

'Gorenflot,' said her husband, 'go out to the carriage-house and get some bricks, and bring in enough to wall up the door of this closet; you can use the plaster that I had left over to plaster the wall.' Then beckoning Rosalie and the workman to him, he said in a low tone: 'Look you, Gorenflot, you will sleep here tonight. But tomorrow morning you shall have a passport to go abroad, to a city which I will name to you. I will give you six thousand francs for your journey. You will remain ten years in that city; if you are not satisfied there, you can settle in another city, provided that it is in the same country. You will go by way of Paris, where you will wait for me. There I will give you a guarantee to pay you six thousand francs more on your return, in case you have abided by the conditions of our bargain. At that price you should be willing to keep silent concerning what you have done here tonight. As

for you, Rosalie, I will give you ten thousand francs, which
will be paid to you on the day of your wedding, provided that
you marry Gorenflot; but, in order to be married, you will
have to be silent; if not, no dower.'

'Rosalie,' said Madame de Merret, 'come here and arrange
my hair.'

The husband walked tranquilly back and forth, watching
the door, the mason, and his wife, but without any outward
sign of injurious suspicion. Gorenflot was obliged to make a
noise; Madame de Merret seized an opportunity, when the
workman was dropping some bricks, and when her husband
was at the other end of the room, to say to Rosalie:

'A thousand francs a year to you, my dear child, if you can
tell Gorenflot to leave a crack at the bottom. – Go and help
him,' she said coolly, aloud.

Monsieur and Madame de Merret said not a word while
Gorenflot was walling up the door. That silence was the result
of design on the husband's part, for he did not choose to allow
his wife a pretext for uttering words of double meaning; and
on Madame de Merret's part, it was either prudence or pride.
When the wall was half built, the crafty mason seized a
moment when the gentleman's back was turned, to strike his
pickaxe through one of the panes of the glass door.

At four o'clock, about daybreak, for it was September, the
work was finished. The mason remained in the house under
the eye of Jean, and Monsieur de Merret slept in his wife's
chamber. In the morning, on rising, he said carelessly:

'Ah! by the way, I must go to the mayor's office, for the
passport.'

He put his hat on his head, walked towards the door, turned
back and took the crucifix. His wife fairly trembled with joy.

'He will go to Duvivier's,' she thought.

As soon as the gentleman had left the room, Madame de
Merret rang for Rosalie; then, in a terrible voice, she cried:

'The pickaxe, the pickaxe! and to work! I saw how Gorenflot understood last night; we shall have time to make a
hole, and stop it up.'

In a twinkling Rosalie brought her mistress a sort of small
axe, and she, with an ardour which no words can describe,
began to demolish the wall. She had already loosened several

bricks, when, as she stepped back to deal a blow even harder than the preceding ones, she saw Monsieur de Merret behind her; she fainted.

'Put madame on her bed,' said the gentleman coldly.

Anticipating what was likely to happen during his absence, he had laid a trap for his wife; he had simply written to the mayor, and had sent a messenger to Duvivier. The jeweller arrived just as the disorder in the room had been repaired.

'Duvivier,' asked Monsieur de Merret, 'didn't you buy some crucifixes from the Spaniards who passed through here?'

'No, monsieur.'

'Very well, I thank you,' he said, exchanging with his wife a tiger-like glance. – 'Jean,' he added, turning towards his confidential valet, 'you will have my meals served in Madame de Merret's room; she is ill, and I shall not leave her until she is well again.'

The cruel man remained with his wife twenty days. During the first days, when there was a noise in the walled-up closet and Josephine attempted to implore him on behalf of the dying unknown, he replied, not allowing her to utter a word:

'You have sworn on the cross that there was no one there.'

EL VERDUGO

EL VERDUGO

Midnight had just sounded from the belfry tower of the little town of Menda. A young French officer, leaning over the parapet of the long terrace at the farther end of the castle gardens, seemed to be unusually absorbed in deep thought for one who led the reckless life of a soldier; but it must be admitted that never were the hour, the scene, and the night more favourable to meditation.

The blue dome of the cloudless sky of Spain was overhead; he was looking out over the coy windings of a lovely valley lit by the uncertain starlight and the soft radiance of the moon. The officer, leaning against an orange tree in blossom, could also see, a hundred feet below him, the town of Menda, which seemed to nestle for shelter from the north wind at the foot of the crags on which the castle itself was built. He turned his head and caught sight of the sea; the moonlit waves made a broad frame of silver for the landscape.

There were lights in the castle windows. The mirth and movement of a ball, the sounds of the violins, the laughter of the officers and their partners in the dance were borne towards him, and blended with the far-off murmur of the waves. The cool night had a certain bracing effect upon his frame, wearied as he had been by the heat of the day. He seemed to bathe in the air, made fragrant by the strong, sweet scent of flowers and of aromatic trees in the gardens.

The castle of Menda belonged to a Spanish grandee, who was living in it at that time with his family. All through the evening the elder daughter of the house had watched the officer with such a wistful interest that the Spanish lady's compassionate eyes might well have set the young Frenchman dreaming. Clara was beautiful; and although she had three brothers and a sister, the broad lands of the Marqués de Légañès appeared to be sufficient warrant for Victor Marchand's belief that the young lady would have a splendid dowry. But how could he dare to imagine that the most fanatical believer in blue blood in all Spain would give his daughter to the son of a grocer in Paris? Moreover, the French were hated. It was because the Marquis had been suspected of an attempt to raise the country in favour of Ferdinand VII that General G——, who governed the province, had stationed Victor Marchand's battalion in the little town of Menda to overawe the neighbouring districts, which received the Marqués de Légañès' word as law. A recent despatch from Marshal Ney had given ground for fear that the English might ere long effect a landing on the coast, and had indicated the Marquis as being in correspondence with the Cabinet in London.

In spite, therefore, of the welcome with which the Spaniards had received Victor Marchand and his soldiers, that officer was always on his guard. As he went towards the terrace, where he had just surveyed the town and the districts confided to his charge, he had been asking himself what construction he ought to put upon the friendliness which the Marquis had invariably shown him, and how to reconcile the apparent tranquillity of the country with his General's uneasiness. But a moment later these thoughts were driven from his mind by the instinct of caution and very legitimate curiosity. It had just struck him that there was a very fair number of lights in the town below. Although it was the Feast of Saint James, he himself had issued orders that very morning that all lights must be put out in the town at the hour prescribed by military regulations. The castle alone had been excepted in this order. Plainly here and there he saw the gleam of bayonets, where his own men were at their accustomed posts; but in the town there was a solemn silence, and not a sign that the Spaniards had given themselves up to the intoxication of a festival. He tried vainly for a while to explain this breach of the regulations on the part of the inhabitants; the mystery seemed but so much the more obscure because he had left instructions with some of his officers to do police duty that night, and make the rounds of the town.

With the impetuosity of youth, he was about to spring through a gap in the wall preparatory to a rapid scramble down the rocks, thinking to reach a small guard-house at the nearest entrance into the town more quickly than by the beaten track, when a faint sound stopped him. He fancied that he could hear the light footstep of a woman along the gravelled garden walk. He turned his head and saw no one; for one moment his eyes were dazzled by the wonderful brightness of the sea, the next he saw a sight so ominous that he stood stock-still with amazement, thinking that his senses must be deceiving him. The white moonbeams lighted the horizon, so that he could distinguish the sails of ships still a considerable distance out at sea. A shudder ran through him; he tried to persuade himself that this was some optical delusion brought about by chance effects of moonlight on the waves; and even as he made the attempt, a hoarse voice called to him by name. The officer glanced at the gap in the wall; saw a soldier's head slowly emerge from it, and recognised the grenadier whom he had ordered to accompany him to the castle.

'Is that you, Commandant?'

'Yes. What is it?' returned the young officer in a low voice. A kind of presentiment warned him to act cautiously.

'Those beggars down there are creeping about like worms; and, by your leave, I came as quickly as I could to report my little reconnoitring expedition.'

'Go on,' answered Victor Marchand.

'I have just been following a man from the castle who came round this way with a lantern in his hand. A lantern is a suspicious matter with a vengeance! I don't imagine that there was any need for that good Christian to be lighting tapers at this time of night. Says I to myself, "They mean to gobble us up!" and I set myself to dogging his heels; and that is how I found out that there is a pile of faggots, sir, two or three steps away from here.'

Suddenly a dreadful shriek rang through the town below, and cut the man short. A light flashed in the Commandant's face, and the poor grenadier dropped down with a bullet through his head. Ten paces away a bonfire flared up like a conflagration. The sounds of music and laughter ceased all at once in the ballroom; the silence of death, broken only by groans, succeeded to the rhythmical murmur of the festival. Then the roar of cannon sounded from across the white plain of the sea.

A cold sweat broke out on the young officer's forehead. He had left his sword behind. He knew that his men had been murdered, and that the English were about to land. He knew that if he lived he would be dishonoured; he saw himself summoned before a court-martial. For a moment his eyes measured the depth of the valley; the next, just as he was about to spring down, Clara's hand caught his.

'Fly!' she cried. 'My brothers are coming after me to kill you. Down yonder at the foot of the cliff you will find Juanito's Andalusian. Go!'

She thrust him away. The young man gazed at her in dull bewilderment; but obeying the instinct of self-preservation, which never deserts even the bravest, he rushed across the park in the direction pointed out to him, springing from rock to rock in places unknown to any save the goats. He heard Clara calling to her brothers to pursue him; he heard the footsteps of the murderers; again and again he heard their balls whistling about his ears; but he reached the foot of the cliff, found the horse, mounted, and fled with lightning speed.

A few hours later the young officer reached General G——'s quarters, and found him at dinner with the staff.

'I put my life in your hands!' cried the haggard and exhausted Commandant of Menda.

He sank into a seat, and told his horrible story. It was received with an appalling silence.

'It seems to me that you are more to be pitied than to blame,' the terrible General said at last. 'You are not answerable for the Spaniard's crimes, and unless the Marshal decides otherwise, I acquit you.'

These words brought but cold comfort to the unfortunate officer.

'When the Emperor comes to hear about it!' he cried.

'Oh, he will be for having you shot,' said the General, 'but we shall see. Now we will say no more about this,' he added severely, 'except to plan a revenge that shall strike a salutary terror into this country, where they carry on war like savages.'

An hour later a whole regiment, a detachment of cavalry, and a convoy of artillery were upon the road. The General and Victor marched at the head of the column. The soldiers had been told of the fate of their comrades, and their rage knew no bounds. The distance between headquarters and the town of Menda was crossed at a well-nigh miraculous speed. Whole villages by the way were found to be under arms; every one of the wretched hamlets was surrounded, and their inhabitants decimated.

It so chanced that the English vessels still lay out at sea, and were no nearer the shore, a fact inexplicable until it was known afterwards that they were artillery transports which had outsailed the rest of the fleet. So the townsmen of Menda, left without the assistance on which they had reckoned when the sails of the English appeared, were surrounded by French troops almost before they had had time to strike a blow. This struck such terror into them that they offered to surrender at discretion. An impulse of devotion, no isolated instance in the history of the Peninsula, led the actual slayers of the French to offer to give themselves up; seeking in this way to save the town, for from the General's reputation for cruelty it was feared that he would give Menda over to the flames, and put the whole population to the sword. General G—— took their offer, stipulating that every soul in the castle from the lowest servant to the Marquis should likewise be given up to him. These terms being accepted, the General promised to spare the lives of the rest of the townsmen, and to prohibit his soldiers from pillaging or setting fire to the town. A heavy contribution was levied, and the wealthiest inhabitants were taken as hostages to guarantee payment within twenty-four hours.

The General took every necessary precaution for the saftey of his troops, provided for the defence of the place, and refused to billet his men in the houses of the town. After they had bivouacked, he went up to the castle and entered it as a conqueror. The whole family of Légañès and their household were gagged, shut up in the great ballroom, and closely watched. From the windows it was easy to see the whole length of the terrace above the town.

The staff was established in an adjoining gallery, where the General forthwith held a council as to the best means of preventing the landing of the English. An aide-de-camp was despatched to Marshal Ney, orders were issued to plant batteries along the coast, and then the General and his staff

turned their attention to their prisoners. The two hundred
Spaniards given up by the townsfolk were shot down then and
there upon the terrace. And after this military execution, the
General gave orders to erect gibbets to the number of the
prisoners in the ballroom in the same place, and to send for the
hangman out of the town. Victor took advantage of the
interval before dinner to pay a visit to the prisoners. He soon
came back to the General.

'I am come in haste,' he faltered out, 'to ask a favour.'

'*You!*' exclaimed the General, with bitter irony in his tones.

'Alas!' answered Victor, 'it is a sorry favour. The Marquis
has seen them erecting the gallows, and hopes that you will
commute the punishment for his family; he entreats you to
have the nobles beheaded.'

'Granted,' said the General.

'He further asks that they may be allowed the consolation of
religion, and that they may be unbound; they give you their
word that they will not attempt to escape.'

'That I permit,' said the General, 'but you are answerable
for them.'

'The old noble offers you all that he has if you will pardon
his youngest son.'

'Really!' cried the Commander. 'His property is forfeit
already to King Joseph.' He paused; a contemptuous thought
set wrinkles in his forehead, as he added, 'I will do better than
they ask. I understand what he means by that last request of
his. Very good. Let him hand down his name to posterity; but
whenever it is mentioned, all Spain shall remember his treason
and its punishment! I will give the fortune and his life to any
one of the sons who will do the executioner's office. . . .
There, don't talk any more about them to me.'

Dinner was ready. The officers sat down to satisfy an
appetite whetted by hunger. Only one among them was
absent from the table – that one was Victor Marchand. After
long hesitation he went to the ballroom, and heard the last
sighs of the proud house of Léganès. He looked sadly at the
scene before him. Only last night, in this very room, he had
seen their faces whirled past him in the waltz, and he
shuddered to think that those girlish heads, with those of the
three young brothers, must fall in a brief space by the

executioner's sword. There sat the father and mother, their three sons and two daughters, perfectly motionless, bound to their gilded chairs. Eight serving men stood with their hands tied behind them. These fifteen prisoners, under sentence of death, exchanged grave glances; it was difficult to read the thoughts that filled them from their eyes, but profound resignation and regret that their enterprise should have failed so completely was written on more than one brow.

The impassive soldiers who guarded them respected the grief of their bitter enemies. A gleam of curiosity lighted up all faces when Victor came in. He gave orders that the condemned prisoners should be unbound, and himself unfastened the cords that held Clara a prisoner. She smiled mournfully at him. The officer could not refrain from lightly touching the young girl's arm; he could not help admiring her dark hair, her slender waist. She was a true daughter of Spain, with a Spanish complexion, a Spaniard's eyes, blacker than the raven's wing beneath their long curving lashes.

'Did you succeed?' she asked, with a mournful smile, in which a certain girlish charm still lingered.

Victor could not repress a groan. He looked from the faces of the three brothers to Clara, and again at the three young Spaniards. The first, the oldest of the family, was a man of thirty. He was short, and somewhat ill made; he looked haughty and proud, but a certain distinction was not lacking in his bearing, and he was apparently no stranger to the delicacy of feeling for which in olden times the chivalry of Spain was famous. His name was Juanito. The second son, Felipe, was about twenty years of age; he was like his sister Clara; and the youngest was a child of eight. In the features of the little Manuel a painter would have discerned something of that Roman steadfastness which David has given to the children's faces in his Republican *genre* pictures. The old Marquis, with his white hair, might have come down from some canvas of Murillo's. Victor threw back his head in despair after this survey; how should one of these accept the General's offer! Nevertheless he ventured to intrust it to Clara. A shudder ran through the Spanish girl, but she recovered herself almost instantly, and knelt before her father.

'Father,' she said, 'bid Juanito swear to obey the commands that you shall give him, and we shall be content.'

The Marquesa trembled with hope, but as she leant towards her husband and learned Clara's hideous secret, the mother fainted away. Juanito understood it all, and leapt up like a caged lion. Victor took it upon himself to dismiss the soldiers, after receiving an assurance of entire submission from the Marquis. The servants were led away and given over to the hangman and their fate. When only Victor remained on guard in the room, the old Marqués de Légañès rose to his feet.

'Juanito,' he said. For all answer Juanito bowed his head in a way that meant refusal; he sank down into his chair, and fixed tearless eyes upon his father and mother in an intolerable gaze. Clara went over to him and sat on his knee; she put her arms about him, and pressed kisses on his eyelids, saying gaily:

'Dear Juanito, if you but knew how sweet death at your hands will be to me! I shall not be compelled to submit to the hateful touch of the hangman's fingers. You will snatch me away from the evils to come and . . . Dear, kind Juanito, you could not bear the thought of my belonging to any one – well, then?'

The velvet eyes gave Victor a burning glance; she seemed to try to awaken in Juanito's heart his hatred for the French.

'Take courage,' said his brother Felipe, 'or our well-nigh royal line will be extinct.'

Suddenly Clara sprang to her feet. The group round Juanito fell back, and the son who had rebelled with such good reason was confronted with his aged father.

'Juanito, I command you!' said the Marquis solemnly.

The young Count gave no sign, and his father fell on his knees; Clara, Manuel, and Felipe unconsciously followed his example, stretching out suppliant hands to him who must save their family from oblivion, and seeming to echo their father's words.

'Can it be that you lack the fortitude of a Spaniard and true sensibility, my son? Do you mean to keep me on my knees? What right have you to think of your own life and of your own sufferings? – Is this my son, madam?' the old Marquis added, turning to his wife.

'He will consent to it,' cried the mother in agony of soul. She had seen a slight contraction of Juanito's brows which she, his mother, alone understood.

Mariquita, the second daughter, knelt, with her slender clinging arms about her mother; the hot tears fell from her eyes, and her little brother Manuel upbraided her for weeping. Just at that moment the castle chaplain came in; the whole family surrounded him and led him up to Juanito. Victor felt that he could endure the sight no longer, and with a sign to Clara he hurried from the room to make one last effort for them. He found the General in boisterous spirits; the officers were still sitting over their dinner and drinking together; the wine had loosened their tongues.

An hour later, a hundred of the principal citizens of Menda were summoned to the terrace by the General's orders to witness the execution of the family of Légañès. A detachment had been told off to keep order among the Spanish townsfolk, who were marshalled beneath the gallows whereon the Marquis's servants hung; the feet of those martyrs of their cause all but touched the citizens' heads. Thirty paces away stood the block; the blade of a scimitar glittered upon it, and the executioner stood by in case Juanito should refuse at the last.

The deepest silence prevailed, but before long it was broken by the sound of many footsteps, the measured tramp of a picket of soldiers, and the jingling of their weapons. Mingled with these came other noises – loud talk and laughter from the dinner-table where the officers were sitting; just as the music and the sound of the dancers' feet had drowned the preparations for last night's treacherous butchery.

All eyes turned to the castle, and beheld the family of nobles coming forth with incredible composure to their death. Every brow was serene and calm. One alone among them, haggard and overcome, leant on the arm of the priest, who poured forth all the consolations of religion for the one man who was condemned to live. Then the executioner, like the spectators, knew that Juanito had consented to perform his office for a day. The old Marquis and his wife, Clara and Mariquita, and their two brothers knelt a few paces from the fatal spot. Juanito reached it, guided by the priest. As he stood at the block the executioner plucked him by the sleeve, and took him aside, probably to give him certain instructions. The confessor so placed the victims that they could not witness the executions, but one and all stood upright and fearless, like Spaniards, as they were.

Clara sprang to her brother's side before the others.

'Juanito,' she said to him, 'be merciful to my lack of courage. Take me first!'

As she spoke, the footsteps of a man running at full speed echoed from the walls, and Victor appeared upon the scene. Clara was kneeling before the block; her white neck seemed to appeal to the blade to fall. The officer turned faint, but he found strength to rush to her side.

'The General grants you your life if you will consent to marry me,' he murmured.

The Spanish girl gave the officer a glance full of proud disdain.

'Now, Juanito!' she said in her deep-toned voice.

Her head fell at Victor's feet. A shudder ran through the Marquesa de Légañès, a convulsive tremor that she could not control, but she gave no other sign of her anguish.

'Is this where I ought to be, dear Juanito? Is it all right?' little Manuel asked his brother.

'Oh, Mariquita, you are weeping!' Juanito said when his sister came.

'Yes,' said the girl; 'I am thinking of you, poor Juanito; how unhappy you will be when we are gone.'

Then the Marquis's tall figure approached. He looked at the block where his children's blood had been shed, turned to the mute and motionless crowd, and said in a loud voice as he stretched out his hands to Juanito:

'Spaniards! I give my son a father's blessing. Now, *Marquis*, strike "without fear"; thou art "without reproach."'

But when his mother came near, leaning on the confessor's arm – 'She fed me from her breast!' Juanito cried, in tones that drew a cry of horror from the crowd. The uproarious mirth of the officers over their wine died away before that terrible cry. The Marquesa knew that Juanito's courage was exhausted; at one bound she sprang to the balustrade, leapt forth, and was dashed to pieces on the rocks below. A cry of admiration broke from the spectators. Juanito swooned.

'General,' said an officer, half drunk by this time, 'Marchand has just been telling me something about this execution; I will wager that it was not by your orders —'

'Are you forgetting, gentlemen, that in a month's time five hundred families in France will be in mourning, and that we are still in Spain?' cried General G——. 'Do you want us to leave our bones here?'

But not a man at the table, not even a subaltern, dared to empty his glass after that speech.

In spite of the respect in which all men hold the Marqués de Léganès, in spite of the title of *El Verdugo* (the executioner) conferred upon him as a patent of nobility by the King of Spain, the great noble is consumed by a gnawing grief. He lives a retired life, and seldom appears in public. The burden of his heroic crime weighs heavily upon him, and he seems to wait impatiently till the birth of a second son shall release him, and he may go to join the Shades that never cease to haunt him.

THE ATHEIST'S MASS

THE ATHEIST'S MASS

Doctor Bianchon – a physician to whom science owes a beautiful physiological theory, and who, though still a young man, has won himself a place among the celebrities of the Paris School, a centre of light to which all the doctors of Europe pay homage – practised surgery before devoting himself to medicine. His early studies were directed by one of the greatest surgeons in France, the celebrated Desplein, who was regarded as a luminary of science. Even his enemies admitted that with him was buried a technical skill he could not bequeath to any successor. Like all men of genius he left no heirs. All that was peculiarly his own he carried to the grave with him.

The glory of great surgeons is like that of actors whose work exists only so long as they live, and of whose talent no adequate idea can be formed when they are gone. Actors and surgeons, and also great singers like those artists who increase tenfold the power of music by the way in which they perform it – all these are the heroes of a moment. Desplein is a striking instance of the similarity of the destinies of such transitory geniuses. His name, yesterday so famous, today almost forgotten, will live among the specialists of his own branch of science without being known beyond it.

But is not an unheard-of combination of circumstances required for the name of a learned man to pass from the domain of science into the general history of mankind? Had Desplein that universality of acquirements that makes of a man the expression, the type of a century? He was gifted with a magnificent power of diagnosis. He could see into the patient and his malady by an acquired or natural intuition, that enabled him to grasp the peculiar characteristics of the individual, and determine the precise moment, the hour, the minute, when he should operate, taking into account both atmospheric conditions and the special temperament of his patient. In order thus to be able to work hand in hand with Nature, had he studied the ceaseless union of organised and elementary substances contained in the atmosphere, or supplied by the earth to man, who absorbs and modifies them so as to derive from them an individual result? Or did he proceed by that power of deduction and analogy to which the genius of Cuvier owed so much?

However that may be, this man had made himself master of all the secrets of the body. He knew it in its past as in its future, taking the present for his point of departure. But did he embody·in his own person all the science of his time, as was the case with Hippocrates, Galen, and Aristotle? Did he lead a whole school towards new worlds of knowledge? No. And while it is impossible to deny to this indefatigable observer of the chemistry of the human body the possession of something like the ancient science of Magism – that is to say, the knowledge of principles in combination, of the causes of life, of life as an antecedent of life, and what it will be through the action of causes preceding its existence – it must be acknowledged that all this was entirely personal to him. Isolated during his life by egotism, this egotism was the suicide of his fame. His tomb is not surmounted by a pretentious statue proclaiming to the future the mysteries that genius has unveiled for it.

But perhaps the talents of Desplein were linked with his beliefs, and therefore mortal. For him the earth's atmosphere was a kind of envelope generating all things. He regarded the earth as an egg in its shell, and unable to solve the old riddle as to whether the egg or the hen came first, he admitted neither the hen nor the egg. He believed neither in a mere animal nature giving origin to the race of man, nor in a spirit surviving him. Desplein was not in doubt. He asserted his theories. His plain open atheism was like that of many men, some of the best fellows in the world, but invincibly atheistic – atheists of a type of which religious people do not admit the existence. This opinion could hardly be otherwise with a man accustomed from his youth to dissect the highest of beings, before, during, and after life, without finding therein that one soul that is so necessary to religious theories. He recognised there a cerebral centre, a nervous centre, and a centre for the respiratory and circulatory system, and the two former so completely supplemented each other, that during the last part of his life he had the conviction that the sense of hearing was not absolutely necessary for one to hear, nor the sense of vision absolutely necessary for sight, and that the solar plexus could replace them without one being aware of the fact. Desplein, recognising these two souls in man, made it an argument for his atheism, without however assuming anything as to the belief in God. This man was said to have died in final impenitence, as many great geniuses have unfortunately died, whom may God forgive.

Great as the man was, his life had in it many 'littlenesses' (to adopt the expression used by his enemies, who were eager to diminish his fame), though it would perhaps be more fitting to call them apparent contradictions. Failing to understand the motives on which high minds act, envious and stupid people at once seize hold of any surface discrepancies to base upon them an indictment, on which they straightway ask for judgment. If, after all, success crowns the methods they have attacked, and shows the co-ordination of preparation and result, all the same something will remain of these charges flung out in advance. Thus in our time Napoleon was condemned by his contemporaries for having spread the wings of the eagle towards England. They had to wait till 1822 for the explanation of 1804, and of the flat-bottomed boats of Boulogne.

In the case of Desplein, his fame and his scientific knowledge not being open to attack, his enemies found fault with his strange whims, his singular character. For he possessed in no small degree that quality which the English call 'eccentricity.' Now he would be attired with a splendour that suggested Crébillon's stately tragedy; and then he would suddenly affect a strange indifference in the matter of dress. One saw him now in a carriage, now on foot. By turns sharp-spoken and kindly; assuming an air of closeness and stinginess, but at the same time ready to put his fortune at the disposal of exiled professors of his science, who would do him the honour of accepting his help for a few days – no one ever gave occasion for more contradictory judgments. Although for the sake of obtaining a decoration that doctors were not allowed to canvass for, he was quite capable of letting a prayer-book slip out of his pocket when at court, you may take it that in his own mind he made a mockery of everything.

He had a deep disdain for men, after having caught glimpses of their true character in the midst of the most solemn and the most trivial acts of their existence. In a great man all his characteristics are generally in keeping with each other. If one of these giants has more talent that wit, it is all the same true that his wit is something deeper than that of one of whom all that can be said is that 'He is a witty fellow.' Genius always implies a certain insight into the moral side of things. This insight may be applied to one special line of thought, but one cannot see the flower without at the same time seeing the sun that produces it. The man who, hearing a diplomatist whom he was saving from death ask, 'How is the Emperor?' remarked, 'The courtier is recovering, and the man will recover with him!' was not merely a doctor or a surgeon, but was also not without a considerable amount of wit. Thus the patient, unwearying observation of mankind might do something to justify the exorbitant pretensions of Desplein, and make one admit that, as he himself believed, he was capable of winning as much distinction as a Minister of State as he had gained as a surgeon.

Amongst the problems that the life of Desplein presented to the minds of his contemporaries, we have chosen one of the most interesting, because the key to it will be found in the ending of the story, and will serve to clear him of many stupid accusations made against him.

Among all Desplein's pupils at the hospital, Horace Bianchon was one of those to whom he was most strongly attached. Before becoming a resident student at the Hôtel Dieu, Horace Bianchon was a medical student, living in the Quartier Latin in a wretched lodging-house, known by the name of Maison Vauquer. There the poor young fellow experienced the pressure of that acute poverty, which is a kind of crucible, whence men of great talent are expected to come forth pure and incorruptible, like a diamond that can be subjected to blows of all kinds without breaking. Though the fierce fire of passion has been aroused, they acquire a probity that it cannot alter, and they become used to struggles that are the lot of genius, in the midst of the ceaseless toil, in which they curb desires that are not to be satisfied. Horace was an upright young man, incapable of taking any crooked course in matters where honour was involved; going straight to the point; ready to pawn his overcoat for his friends, as he was to give them his time and his long vigils. In a word, Horace was one of those friends who do not trouble themselves as to what they are to receive in return for what they bestow, taking it for granted that, when it comes to their turn, they will get more than they give. Most of his friends had for him that heart-felt respect which is inspired by unostentatious worth, and many of them would have been afraid to provoke his censure. But Horace manifested these good qualities without any pedantic display. Neither a puritan nor a preacher, he would in his simplicity enforce a word of good advice with any oath, and was ready for a bit of good cheer when the occasion offered. A pleasant comrade, with no more shyness than a trooper, frank and outspoken – not as a sailor for the sailor of today is a wily diplomatist – but as a fine young fellow, who has nothing in his life to be ashamed of, he went his way with head erect and with a cheerful mind. To sum it all up in one word, Horace was the Pylades of more than one Orestes, creditors nowadays playing most realistically the part of the Furies. He bore his poverty with that gaiety which is perhaps one of the chief elements of courage, and, like all those who have nothing, he contracted very few debts. As enduring as a camel, as alert as a wild deer, he was steadfast in his ideas and in his conduct.

The happiness of Bianchon's life began on the day when the famous surgeon became acquainted with the good qualities and the defects, which, each as well as the other, make Dr. Horace Bianchon doubly dear to his friends. When the teacher of the hospital class receives a young man into his inner circle, that young man has, as the saying goes, his foot in the stirrup. Desplein did not fail to take Bianchon with him as his assistant to wealthy houses, where nearly always a gratuity slipped into the purse of the student, and where, all unconsciously, the young provincial had revealed to him some of the mysteries of Parisian life. Desplein would have him in his study during consultations, and found work for him there. Sometimes he would send him to a watering-place as companion to a rich invalid, – in a word, he was preparing a professional connection for him. The result of all this was that after a certain time the tyrant of the operating theatre had his right-hand man. These two – one of them at the summit of professional honours and science, and in the enjoyment of an immense fortune and an equal renown, the other a modest cipher without fortune or fame – became intimate friends. The great Desplein told everything to his pupil. Bianchon came to know the mysteries of this temperament, half lion, half bull, that in the end caused an abnormal expansion of the great man's chest and killed him by enlargement of the heart. He studied the odd whims of this busy life, the schemes of its sordid avarice, the projects of this politician disguised as a man of science. He was able to forecast the disappointments that awaited the one touch of sentiment that was buried in a heart not of stone though made to seem like stone.

One day Bianchon told Desplein that a poor water-carrier in the Quartier Saint-Jacques was suffering from a horrible illness caused by overwork and poverty. This poor native of Auvergne had only potatoes to eat during the hard winter of 1821. Desplein left all his patients. At the risk of breaking down his horse, he drove at full speed, accompanied by Bianchon, to the poor man's lodging, and himself super-intended his removal to a private nursing home established by the celebrated Dubois in the Faubourg Saint-Denis. He went to attend to the man himself, and gave him, when he had recovered, money enough to buy a horse and a water-cart. The Auvergnat distinguished himself by an unconventional proceeding. One of his friends fell sick, and he at once brought him to Desplein, and said to his benefactor:

'I would not think of allowing him to go to any one else.'

Overwhelmed with work as he was, Desplein grasped the water-carrier's hand and said to him:

'Bring them all to me.'

He had this poor fellow from the Cantal admitted to the Hôtel Dieu, where he took the greatest care of him. Bianchon had on many occasions remarked that his chief had a particular liking for people from Auvergne, and especially for the water-carriers; but as Desplein took a kind of pride in his treatment of his poor patients at the Hôtel Dieu, his pupil did not see anything very strange in this.

One day when Bianchon was crossing the Place Saint-Sulpice he caught sight of his teacher going into the church about nine o'clock in the morning. Desplein, who at this period would not go a step without calling for his carriage, was on foot, and slipped in quietly by the side door in the Rue du Petit Lion, as if he was going into some doubtful place. The student was naturally seized by a great curiosity, for he knew the opinions of his master; so Bianchon too slipped into Saint-Sulpice and was not a little surprised to see the famous Desplein, this atheist, who thought very little of angels, as beings who give no scope for surgery, this scoffer, humbly kneeling, and where? . . . in the Lady Chapel, where he heard a mass, gave an alms for the church expenses and for the poor, and remained throughout as serious as if he were engaged in an operation.

Bianchon's astonishment knew no bounds. 'If,' he said to himself, 'I had seen him holding one of the cords of the canopy at a public procession on Corpus Christi I might just laugh at him; but at this time of day, all alone, without any one to see him, this is certainly something to set one thinking!'

Bianchon had no wish to appear to be playing the spy on the chief surgeon of the Hôtel Dieu, so he went away. It so happened that Desplein asked him to dine with him that day, not at his house but at a restaurant. Between the cheese and dessert Bianchon, by cleverly leading up to it, managed to say something about the mass, and spoke of it as a mummery and a farce.

'A farce,' said Desplein, 'that has cost Christendom more bloodshed than all the battles of Napoleon, all the leeches of Broussais. It is a papal invention, that only dates from the sixth century. What torrents of blood were not shed to establish the feast of Corpus Christi, by which the Court of Rome sought to mark its victory in the question of the real presence, and the schism that has troubled the Church for three centuries! The wars of the Count of Toulouse and the Albigenses were the sequel of that affair. The Vaudois and the Albigenses refused to recognise the innovation.'

In a word Desplein took a pleasure in giving vent to all his atheistic ardour, and there was a torrent of Voltairian witticisms, or, to describe it more accurately, a detestable imitation of the style of the modern anti-clerical journalists.

'Hum!' said Bianchon to himself, 'what has become of my devotee of this morning?'

He kept silent. He began to doubt if it was really his chief that he had seen at Saint-Sulpice. Desplein would not have taken the trouble to lie to Bianchon. They knew each other too well. They had already exchanged ideas on points quite as serious, and discussed systems of the nature of things, exploring and dissecting them with the knives and scalpels of incredulity.

Three months went by. Bianchon took no further step in connection with the incident, though it remained graven in his memory. One day that year one of the doctors of the Hôtel Dieu took Desplein by the arm in Bianchon's presence, as if he had a question to put to him.

'Whatever do you go to Saint-Sulpice for, my dear master?' he said to him.

'To see one of the priests there, who has caries in the knee, and whom Madame the Duchess of Angoulême did me the honour to recommend to my care,' said Desplein.

The doctor was satisfied with this evasion, but not so Bianchon.

'Ah, he goes to see diseased knees in the church! Why, he went to hear mass!' said the student to himself.

Bianchon made up his mind to keep a watch on Desplein. He remembered the day, the hour, when he had caught him going into Saint-Sulpice, and he promised himself that he would be there next year on the same day and at the same hour, to see if he would catch him again. In this case the recurring date of his devotions would give ground for a scientific investigation, for one ought not to expect to find in such a man a direct contradiction between thought and action.

Next year, on the day and at the hour, Bianchon, who by this time was no longer one of Desplein's resident students, saw the surgeon's carriage stop at the corner of the Rue de Tournon and the Rue du Petit Lion. His friend got out, passed stealthily along by the wall of Saint-Sulpice, and once more

heard his mass at the Lady altar. It was indeed Desplein, the
chief surgeon of the hospital, the atheist at heart, the devotee
at haphazard. The problem was getting to be a puzzle. The
persistence of the illustrious man of science made it all very
complicated. When Desplein had gone out Bianchon went up
to the sacristan, who came to do his work in the chapel, and
asked him if that gentleman was a regular attendant there.

'Well, I have been here twenty years,' said the sacristan,
'and all that time M. Desplein has come four times a year to
be present at this mass. He founded it.'

'A foundation made by him!' said Bianchon, as he went
away. 'Well, it is more wonderful than all the mysteries.'

Some time passed by before Dr. Bianchon, although the
friend of Desplein, found an opportunity to talk to him of this
singular incident in his life. Though they met in consultation
or in society, it was difficult to get that moment of
confidential chat alone together, when two men sit with their
feet on the fender, and their heads resting on the backs of their
armchairs, and tell each other their secrets. At last, after a
lapse of seven years, and after the Revolution of 1830, when
the people had stormed the Archbishop's house, when
Republican zeal led them to destroy the gilded crosses that
shone like rays of light above the immense sea of house-tops,
when unbelief side by side with revolt paraded the streets,
Bianchon again came upon Desplein as he entered the church
of Saint-Sulpice. The doctor followed him in, and took his
place beside him, without his friend taking any notice of him,
or showing the least surprise. Together they heard the mass
he had founded.

'Will you tell me, my dear friend,' said Bianchon to
Desplein, when they left the church, 'the reason for this
monkish proceeding of yours? I have already caught you
going to mass three times, you of all men! You must tell me
the meaning of this mystery, and explain to me this flagrant
contradiction between your opinions and your conduct. You
don't believe in God and you go to mass! My dear master,
you are bound to give me an answer.'

'I am like a good many devotees, men deeply religious
to all appearance, but quite as much atheists as we can be,
you and I.'

And then there was a torrent of epigrams referring to certain political personages, the best known of whom presents us in our own time with a new edition of the *Tartuffe* of Molière.

'I am not asking you about all that,' said Bianchon. 'But I do want to know the reason for what you have just been doing here. Why have you founded this mass?'

'My word! my dear friend,' said Desplein, 'I am on the brink of the grave, and I may just as well talk to you about the early days of my life.'

Just then Bianchon and the great man were in the Rue des Quatre Vents, one of the most horrible streets in Paris. Desplein pointed to the sixth storey of one of those high, narrow-fronted houses that stand like obelisks. The outer door opens on a passage, at the end of which is a crooked stair, lighted by small inner windows. It was a house with a greenish-coloured front, with a furniture dealer installed on the ground floor, and apparently a different type of wretchedness lodging in every storey. As he raised his arm with a gesture that was full of energy, Desplein said to Bianchon:

'I lived up there for two years!'

'I know that. D'Arthez used to live there. I came there nearly every day when I was quite a young fellow, and in those days we used to call it "the store bottle of great men!" Well, what comes next?'

'The mass that I have just heard is connected with events that occurred when I was living in that garret in which you tell me D'Arthez once lived, the room from the window of which there is a line hanging with clothes drying on it, just above the flower-pot. I had such a rough start in life, my dear Bianchon, that I could dispute with any one you like the palm for suffering endured here in Paris. I bore it all, hunger, thirst, want of money, lack of clothes, boots, linen – all that is hardest in poverty. I have tried to warm my frozen fingers with my breath in that "store bottle of great men," which I should like to revisit with you. As I worked in the winter a vapour would rise from my head and I could see the steam of perspiration as we see it about the horses on a frosty day. I don't know where one finds the foothold to stand up against such a life. I was all alone, without help, without a penny to buy books or to pay the expenses of my medical education: without a friend, for my irritable, gloomy, nervous character did me harm.

'No one would recognise in my fits of irritation the distress, the struggles of a man who is striving to rise to the surface from his place in the very depths of the social system. But I can say to you, in whose presence I have no need to cloak myself in any way, that I had that basis of sound ideas and impressionable feelings, which will always be part of the endowment of men strong enough to climb up to some summit, after having long plodded through the morass of misery. I could not look for any help from my family or my native place beyond the insufficient allowance that was made to me. To sum it all up, at that time my breakfast in the morning was a roll that a baker in the Rue du Petit Lion sold cheaply to me because it was from the baking of yesterday or the day before, and which I broke up into some milk; thus my morning meal did not cost me more than a penny. I dined only every second day, in a boarding-house where one could get a dinner for eightpence. Thus I spent only fourpence-halfpenny a day.

'You know as well as I do what care I would take of such things as clothes and boots! I am not sure that in later life we feel more trouble at the treachery of a colleague than we have felt, you and I, at discovering the mocking grimace of a boot-sole that is coming away from the sewing, or at hearing the rending noise of a torn coat-cuff. I drank only water. I looked at the cafés with the greatest respect. The Café Zoppi seemed to me like a promised land, where the Luculluses of the Quartier Latin had the exclusive right of entry. "Shall I ever," I used sometimes to ask myself, "shall I ever be able to go in there to take a cup of coffee and hot milk, or to play a game of dominoes?"

'Well, I brought to my work the furious energy that my poverty inspired. I tried rapidly to get a grasp of exact knowledge so as to acquire an immense personal worth in order to deserve the position I hoped to reach in the days when I would have come forth from my nothingness. I consumed more oil than bread. The lamp that lighted me during these nights of persistent toil cost me more than my food. The struggle was long, obstinate, without encouragement. I had won no sympathy from those around me. To have friends must one not associate with other young fellows, and have a few pence to take a drink with them, and go with them wherever students are to be found? I had nothing. And no one in Paris quite realises that *nothing* is really *nothing*. If I ever had any occasion to reveal my misery I felt in my throat that nervous contraction that makes our patients sometimes imagine there is a round mass coming up the gullet into the larynx. Later on I have come across people who, having been born in wealth and never wanted for anything, knew nothing of that problem of the Rule of Three: A young man is to a crime as a five franc piece is to the unknown quantity X. These gilded fools would say to me:

'"But why do you get into debt? Why ever do you contract serious obligations?"

'They remind me of that princess who, on hearing that the people were in want of bread, said: "Why don't they buy sponge cakes?" I should like very much to see one of those rich men, who complains that I ask him for too high a fee when there has to be an operation – yes, I should like to see him all alone in Paris, without a penny, without luggage, without a friend, without credit, and forced to work his five fingers to the bone to get a living. What would he do? Where would he go to satisfy his hunger? Bianchon, if you have sometimes seen me bitter and hard, it was because I was then thinking at once of my early troubles and of the heartlessness, the selfishness of which I have seen a thousand instances in the highest circles; or else I was thinking of the obstacles that hatred, envy, jealousy, calumny have raised up between me and success. In Paris, when certain people see you ready to put your foot in the stirrup, some of them pull at the skirt of your coat, others loosen the saddle-girth; this one knocks a shoe off your horse, that one steals your whip; the least treacherous of the lot is the one you see coming to fire a pistol at you point blank.

'You have talent enough, my dear fellow, to know soon enough the horrible, the unceasing warfare that mediocrity carries on against the man that is its superior. If one evening you lose twenty-five *louis*, next morning you will be accused of being a gambler, and your best friends will say that you lost twenty-five thousand francs last night. If you have a headache, you will be set down as a lunatic. If you are not lively, you will be set down as unsociable. If to oppose this battalion of pygmies you call up your own superior powers, your best friends will cry out that you wish to devour everything, that you claim to lord it and play the tyrant. In a word, your good qualities will be turned into defects, your defects will be turned into vices, and your virtues will be crimes. If you have saved some one, it will be said that you have killed him. If your patient reappears, it will be agreed that you have made sure of the present at the expense of his future; though he is not dead, he will die. If you stumble, it will be a fall! Invent anything whatever, and assert your rights, and you will be a difficult man to deal with, a sharp fellow, who does not like to see young men succeed. So, my dear friend, if I do not believe in God, I believe even less in man. Do you not recognise in me a Desplein that is quite different from the Desplein about whom every one speaks ill? But we need not dig into that heap of mud.

'Well, I was living in that house, I had to work to be ready to pass my first examination, and I had not a farthing. You know what it is! I had come to one of those crises of utter extremity when one says to oneself: 'I will enlist!' I had one hope. I was expecting from my native place a trunk full of linen, a present from some old aunts, who, knowing nothing of Paris, think about providing one with dress shirts, because they imagine that with thirty francs a month their nephew dines on ortolans. The trunk arrived while I was away at the Medical School. It had cost forty francs, carriage to be paid. The concierge of the house, a German cobbler, who lived in a loft, had paid the money and held the trunk. I took a walk in the Rue des Fosse-Saint-Germain-des-Prés and in the Rue de l'École de Médicine without being able to invent a stratagem which would put the trunk in my possession, without my being obliged to pay down the forty francs, which of course I meant to pay after selling the linen. My stupidity seemed a very fair sign to me that I was fit for no vocation but surgery. My dear friend, delicately organised natures, whose powers are exercised in some higher sphere, are wanting in that spirit

of intrigue which is fertile in resources and shifts. Genius such
as theirs depends on chance. They do not seek out things, they
come upon them.

'At last, after dark, I went back to the house, just at the
moment when my next-room neighbour was coming in, a
water-carrier named Bourgeat, a man from Saint-Flour in
Auvergne. We knew each other in the way in which two
lodgers come to know each other, when both have their rooms
on the same landing, and they can hear each other going to bed,
coughing, getting up, and end by becoming quite used to each
other. My neighbour informed me that the landlord, to whom
I owed three months' rent, had sent me notice to quit. I must
clear out next day. He himself was to be evicted on account of
his business. I passed the most sorrowful night of my life.

'Where was I to find a porter to remove my poor belongings,
my books? How was I to pay the porter and the concierge?
Where could I go? With tears in my eyes I repeated these
insoluble questions, as lunatics repeat their catchwords. I fell
asleep. For the wretched there is a divine sleep full of beautiful
dreams. Next morning, while I was eating my porringer full of
bread crumbled into milk, Bourgeat came in, and said to me in
bad French:

'"Mister Student, I'm a poor man, a foundling of the hospice
of Saint-Flour, without father or mother, and not rich enough
to marry. You are not much better off for relations, or better
provided with what counts? Now, see here, I have down
below a hand-cart that I have hired at a penny an hour. All our
things can be packed on it. If you agree, we will look for a place
where we can lodge together, since we are turned out of this.
And after all, it's not the earthly paradise."

'"I know it well, my good Bourgeat," said I to him, "but I
am in a great difficulty. There's a trunk for me downstairs that
contains linen worth a hundred crowns, with which I could
pay the landlord and what I owe to the concierge, and I have
not got as much as a hundred sous."

'"Bah! I have found some bits of coin," Bourgeat answered
me joyfully, showing me an old purse of greasy leather. "Keep
your linen."

'Bourgeat paid my three months, and his own rent, and
settled with the concierge. Then he put our furniture and my

box of linen on his hand-cart and drew it through the streets, stopping at every house that showed a "Lodgings to Let" card. As for me I would go upstairs to see if the place to let would suit us. At noon we were still wandering about the Quartier Latin without having found anything. The rent was the great obstacle. Bourgeat proposed to me to have lunch at a wine-shop, at the door of which we left the hand-cart. Towards evening, in the Cour de Rohan off the Passage du Commerce, I found, under the roof at the top of a house, two rooms, one on each side of the staircase. We got them for a rent of sixty francs a year each. So there we were housed, myself and my humble friend.

'We dined together. Bourgeat, who earned some fifty sous a day, had saved about a hundred crowns. . . . He would soon be in a position to realise his ambition and buy a water-cart and a horse. When he found out how I was situated – and he wormed out my secrets with a depth of cunning and at the same time with a kindly good nature that still moves my heart today when I think of it – he renounced for some time to come the ambition of his life. Bourgeat had been a street seller for twenty-two years. He sacrificed his hundred crowns for my future.'

At this point Desplein took a firm grip of Bianchon's arm.

'He gave me the money required for my examinations! This man understood, my friend, that I had a mission, that the needs of my intelligence came before his. He busied himself with me, he called me his "little one," he lent me the money I wanted to buy books; he came in sometimes quite quietly to watch me at my work; finally he took quite a motherly care to see that I substituted a wholesome and abundant diet for the bad and insufficient fare to which I had been condemned. Bourgeat, a man of about forty, had the features of a burgess of the middle ages, a full rounded forehead, a head that a painter might have posed as the model for a Lycurgus. The poor man felt his heart big with affection seeking for some object. He had never been loved by anything but a poodle, that had died a short time before, and about which he was always talking to me, asking if by any possibility the Church would consent to have prayers for its soul. His dog, he said, had been really like a Christian, and for twelve years it had gone to church with him, without ever barking, listening to the organ without so much as opening its mouth, and remaining crouched beside him with a look that made one think it was praying with him.

'This man transferred all his affection to me. He took me up as a lonely, suffering creature. He became for me like a most watchful mother, the most delicately thoughtful of benefactors, in a word the ideal of that virtue that rejoices in its own good work. When I met him in the street he gave me an intelligent look, full of a nobility that you cannot imagine; he would then assume a gait like that of a man who was carrying no burden; he seemed delighted at seeing me in good health and well dressed. It was such devoted affection as one finds among the common people, the love of the little shop-girl raised to a higher level. Bourgeat ran my errands. He woke me up in the night at the appointed hour. He trimmed my lamp, scrubbed our landing. He was a good servant as well as a good father to me, and as cleanly in his work as an English maid. He looked after our housekeeping. Like Philopoemen he sawed up our firewood, and he set about all his actions with a simplicity in performing them that at the same time preserved his dignity, for he seemed to realise that the end in view ennobled it all.

'When I left this fine fellow to enter the Hôtel Dieu as a resident student, he felt a kind of sorrowful gloom come over him at the thought that he could no longer live with me. But he consoled himself by looking forward to getting together the money that would be necessary for the expenses of my final examination, and he made me promise to come to see him on all my holidays. Bourgeat was proud of me. He loved me for my own sake and for his own. If you look up my essay for the doctorate you will see that it was dedicated to him. In the last year of my indoor course I had made enough money to be able to repay all I owed to this worthy Auvergnat, by buying him a horse and a water-cart. He was exceedingly angry at finding that I was thus depriving myself of my money, and nevertheless he was delighted at seeing his desires realised. He laughed and he scolded me. He looked at his water-barrel and his horse, and he wiped away a tear as he said to me:

'"It's a pity! Oh, what a fine water-cart! You have done
wrong! . . . The horse is as strong as if he came from
Auvergne!"

'He absolutely insisted on buying for me that pocket-case of
instruments mounted with silver that you have seen in my
study, and which is for me the most valued of my possessions.
Although he was enraptured with my first successes he never
let slip a word or a gesture that could be taken to mean, "It is
to me that this man's success is due!" And nevertheless, but for
him, I should have been killed by my misery. The poor man
broke himself down for my sake. He had eaten nothing but
bread seasoned with garlic, in order that I might have coffee
while I sat up at my work. He fell sick. You may imagine how
I passed whole nights at his bedside. I pulled him through it
the first time, but two years after there was a relapse, and
notwithstanding the most assiduous care, notwithstanding the
greatest efforts of science, he had to succumb. No king was
ever cared for as he was. Yes, Bianchon, to snatch this life
from death I tried unheard-of things. I wanted to make him
live long enough to allow him to see the results of his work, to
realise all his wishes, to satisfy the one gratitude that had filled
my heart, to extinguish a fire that burned in me even now!'

'Bourgeat,' continued Desplein, after a pause, with evident
emotion, 'Bourgeat, my second father, died in my arms,
leaving me all he possessed by a will which he had made at a
public notary's, and which bore the date of the year when we
went to lodge in the Cour de Rohan. He had the faith of a
simple workman. He loved the Blessed Virgin as he would
have loved his mother. Zealous Catholic as he was, he had
never said a word to me about my own lack of religion. When
he was in danger of death he begged me to spare nothing to
obtain the help of the Church for him. I had mass said for him
every day. Often in the night he expressed to me his fears for
his future; he was afraid that he had not lived a holy enough
life. Poor man! he used to work from morning to night. Who
is heaven for, then, if there is a heaven? He received the last
sacraments like the saint that he was, and his death was
worthy of his life.

'I was the only one who followed his funeral. When I had
laid my one benefactor in the earth, I tried to find out how I

could discharge my debt of gratitude to him. I knew that he had neither family nor friends, neither wife nor children. But he believed! He had religious convictions, and had I any right to dispute them? He had spoken to me timidly of masses said for the repose of the dead; he did not seek to impose this duty on me, thinking that it would be like asking to be paid for his services to me. As soon as I could arrange for the endowment, I gave the Saint-Sulpice the sum necessary to have four masses said there each year. As the only thing that I could offer to Bourgeat was the fulfilment of his pious wishes, I go there in his name on the day the mass is said at the beginning of each quarter of the year, and say the prayers for him that he wished for. I say them in the good faith of one who doubts: "My God, if there is a sphere where after their death you place those who have been perfect, think of good Bourgeat; and if he has still anything to suffer, lay these sufferings on me, so that he may enter the sooner into what they call Paradise!" This, my dear friend, is all that a man who holds my opinions can allow himself. God must be good-hearted, and He will not take it ill on my part. But I swear to you, I would give my fortune for the sake of finding the faith of Bourgeat coming into my brain.'

Bianchon, who attended Desplein in his last illness, does not venture to affirm, even now, that the famous surgeon died an atheist. Will not those who believe take pleasure in the thought that perhaps the poor Auvergnat came to open for him the gate of Heaven, as he had already opened for him the portals of that temple on earth, on the façade of which one reads: *To great men from their grateful motherland*?

A SEASHORE DRAMA

A SEASHORE DRAMA

Young men almost always have a pair of compasses with which they delight to measure the future; when their will is in accord with the size of the angle which they make, the world is theirs. But this phenomenon of moral life takes place only at a certain age. That age, which in the case of all men comes between the years of twenty-two and twenty-eight, is the age of noble thoughts, the age of first conceptions, because it is the age of unbounded desires, the age at which one doubts nothing; he who talks of doubt speaks of impotence. After that age, which passes as quickly as the season for sowing, comes the age of execution. There are in a certain sense two youths: one during which one thinks, the other during which one acts; often they are blended, in men whom nature has favoured, and who, like Caesar, Newton, and Bonaparte, are the greatest among great men.

I was reckoning how much time a thought needs to develop itself; and, compasses in hand, standing on a cliff a hundred fathoms above the ocean, whose waves played among the reefs, I laid out my future, furnishing it with works, as an engineer draws fortresses and palaces upon vacant land. The sea was lovely; I had just dressed after bathing; I was waiting for Pauline, my guardian angel, who was bathing in a granite bowl full of white sand, the daintiest bath-tub that Nature ever designed for any of her sea-fairies. We were at the extreme point of Le Croisic, a tiny peninsula of Brittany; we were far from the harbour, in a spot which the authorities considered so inaccessible that the customs officers almost never visited it. To swim in the air after swimming in the sea! Ah! who would not have swum into the future? Why did I think? Why does evil happen? Who knows? Ideas come to your heart, or your brain, without consulting you. No courtesan was ever more whimsical or more imperious than is conception in an artist; it must be caught, like fortune, by the hair, when it comes. Clinging to my thought, as Astolpho clung to his hippogriff, I galloped through the world, arranging everything therein to suit my pleasure.

When I looked about me in search of some omen favourable to the audacious schemes which my wild imagination advised me to undertake, a sweet cry, the cry of a woman calling in the silence of the desert, the cry of a woman coming from the bath, refreshed and joyous, drowned the murmur of the fringe of foam tossed constantly back and forth by the rising and falling of the waves in the indentations of the shore. When I heard that note, uttered by the soul, I fancied that I had seen on the cliff the foot of an angel, who, as she unfolded her wings, had called to me: 'Thou shalt have success!' I descended, radiant with joy and light as air; I went bounding down, like a stone down a steep slope. When she saw me, she said to me: 'What is the matter?' I did not answer, but my eyes became moist. The day before, Pauline had understood my pain, as she understood at that moment my joy, with the magical sensitiveness of a harp which follows the variations of the atmosphere. The life of man has some glorious moments! We walked silently along the shore. The sky was cloudless, the sea without a ripple; others would have seen only two blue plains, one above the other; but we who understood each other without need of speech, we who could discover between those two swaddling-cloths of infinity the illusions with which youth is nourished, we pressed each other's hand at the slightest change which took place either in the sheet of water or in the expanse of air; for we took those trivial phenomena for material interpretations of our twofold thought.

Who has not enjoyed that unbounded bliss in pleasures, when the soul seems to be released from the bonds of the flesh, and to be restored as it were to the world whence it came? Pleasure is not our only guide in those regions. Are there not times when the sentiments embrace each other as of their own motion, and fly thither, like two children who take each other's hands and begin to run without knowing why or whither? We walked along thus.

At the moment that the roofs of the town appeared on the horizon, forming a greyish line, we met a poor fisherman who was returning to Le Croisic. His feet were bare, his canvas trousers were ragged on the edges, with many holes imperfectly mended; he wore a shirt of sail-cloth, wretched list suspenders, and his jacket was a mere rag. The sight of that misery distressed us – a discord, as it were, in the midst of our harmony. We looked at each other, to lament that we had not at that moment the power to draw upon the treasury of Abu-l-Kásim. We saw a magnificent lobster and a crab hanging by a cord which the fisherman carried in his right hand, while in the other he had his nets and his fishing apparatus. We accosted him, with the purpose of buying his fish, an idea which occurred to both of us, and which expressed itself in a smile, to which I replied by slightly pressing the arm which I held and drawing it closer to my heart. It was one of those nothings which the memory afterward transforms into a poem, when, sitting by the fire, we recall the time when that nothing moved us, the place where it happened, and that mirage, the effects of which have never been defined, but which often exerts an influence upon the objects which surround us, when life is pleasant and our hearts are full.

The loveliest places are simply what we make them. Who is the man, however little of a poet he may be, who has not in his memory a boulder that occupies more space than the most famous landscape visited at great expense? Beside that boulder what tempestuous thoughts! there, a whole life mapped out; here, fears banished; there, rays of hope entered the heart. At that moment, the sun, sympathising with these thoughts of love and of the future, cast upon the yellowish sides of that cliff an ardent beam; some mountain wild-flowers attracted the attention; the tranquillity and silence magnified that uneven surface, in reality dark of hue, but made brilliant by the dreamer; then it was beautiful, with its meagre vegetation, its warm-hued camomile, its Venus's hair, with the velvety leaves. A prolonged festivity, superb decorations, placid exaltation of human strength! Once before, the Lake of Bienne, seen from Île St.-Pierre, had spoken to me thus; perhaps the cliff of Le Croisic would be the last of those delights. But, in that case, what would become of Pauline?

'You have had fine luck this morning, my good man,' I said to the fisherman.

'Yes, monsieur,' he replied, stopping to turn towards us the tanned face of those who remain for hours at a time exposed to the reflection of the sun on the water.

That face indicated endless resignation; the patience of the fisherman, and his gentle manners. That man had a voice without trace of harshness, kindly lips, no ambition; an indefinably frail and sickly appearance. Any other type of face would have displeased us.

'Where are you going to sell your fish?'

'At the town.'

'How much will you get for the lobster?'

'Fifteen sous.'

'And for the crab?'

'Twenty sous.'

'Why so much difference between the lobster and the crab?'

'The crab is much more delicate, monsieur; and then it's as cunning as a monkey, and don't often allow itself to be caught.'

'Will you let us have both for a hundred sous?' said Pauline. The man was thunderstruck.

'You shan't have them!' I said laughingly; 'I will give ten francs. We must pay for emotions all that they are worth.'

'Very well,' she replied, 'I propose to have them; I will give ten francs two sous.'

'Ten sous.'

'Twelve francs.'

'Fifteen francs.'

'Fifteen francs fifty,' she said.

'One hundred francs.'

'One hundred and fifty.'

I bowed. At that moment we were not rich enough to carry the bidding any farther. The poor fisherman did not know whether he ought to be angry as at a practical joke, or to exult; we relieved him from his dilemma by giving him the name of our landlady and telling him to take the lobster and the crab to her house.

'Do you earn a living?' I asked him, in order to ascertain to what cause his destitution should be attributed.

'With much difficulty and many hardships,' he replied. 'Fishing on the seashore, when you have neither boat nor nets, and can fish only with a line, is a risky trade. You see, you have to wait for the fish or the shell-fish to come, while the fishermen with boats can go out to sea after them. It is so hard to earn a living this way, that I am the only man who fishes on the shore. I pass whole days without catching anything. The only way I get anything is when a crab forgets himself and goes to sleep, as this one did, or a lobster is fool enough to stay on the rocks. Sometimes, after a high sea, the wolf-fish come in, and then I grab them.'

'Well, take one day with another, what do you earn?'

'Eleven or twelve sous. I could get along with that if I were alone; but I have my father to support, and the poor man can't help me, for he's blind.'

At that sentence, uttered with perfect simplicity, Pauline and I looked at each other without a word.

'You have a wife or a sweetheart?'

He cast at us one of the most pitiful glances that I ever saw, as he replied:

'If I had a wife, then I should have to let my father go; I couldn't support him, and a wife and children too.'

'Well, my poor fellow, how is it that you don't try to earn more by carrying salt to the harbour, or by working in the salt marshes?'

'Oh! I couldn't do that for three months, monsieur. I am not strong enough; and if I should die, my father would have to beg. What I must have is a trade that requires very little skill and a great deal of patience.'

'But how can two people live on twelve sous a day?'

'Oh, monsieur, we eat buckwheat cakes, and barnacles that I take off the rocks.'

'How old are you?'

'Thirty-seven.'

'Have you ever been away from here?'

'I went to Guérande once, to draw my lot in the draft, and I went to Savenay, to show myself to some gentlemen who measured me. If I had been an inch taller I should have been drafted. I should have died on the first long march, and my poor father would have been asking alms today.'

I had thought out many dramas; Pauline was accustomed to intense emotions, living with a man in my condition of health;

but neither of us had ever listened to more touching words than those of that fisherman. We walked some distance in silence, both of us measuring the silent depths of that unknown life, admiring the nobility of that self-sacrifice which was unconscious of itself; the strength of his weakness surprised us; that unconscious generosity made us small in our own eyes. I saw that poor creature, all instinct, chained to that rock as a galley-slave is chained to his ball, watching for twenty years for shell-fish to support himself, and sustained in his patience by a single sentiment. How many hours passed on the edge of that beach! how many hopes crushed by a squall, by a change of weather! He hung over the edge of a granite shelf, his arms stretched out like those of an Indian fakir, while his father, sitting on a stool, waited in silence and darkness for him to bring him the coarsest of shell-fish and of bread, if the sea were willing.

'Do you ever drink wine?' I asked him.

'Three or four times a year.'

'Well, you shall drink some today, you and your father, and we will send you a white loaf.'

'You are very kind, monsieur.'

'We will give you your dinner if you will guide us along the shore as far as Batz, where we are going, to see the tower which overlooks the basin and the coast between Batz and Le Croisic.'

'With pleasure,' he said. 'Go straight ahead, follow the road you are now on; I will overtake you after I have got rid of my fish and my tackle.'

We nodded simultaneously, and he hurried off towards the town, light at heart. That meeting held us in the same mental situation in which we were previously, but it had lowered our spirits.

'Poor man!' said Pauline, with that accent which takes away from a woman's compassion whatever there may be offensive in pity; 'does it not make one feel ashamed to be happy when one sees such misery?'

'Nothing is more cruel than to have impotent desires,' I replied. 'Those two poor creatures, father and son, will no more know how keen our sympathy is than the world knows how noble their lives are; for they are laying up treasures in heaven.'

'What a wretched country!' she said, as she pointed out to me, along a field surrounded by a loose stone wall, lumps of cow-dung arranged symmetrically. 'I asked some one what those were. A peasant woman, who was putting them in place, answered that she was *making wood*. Just fancy, my dear, that when these blocks of dung are dried, these poor people gather them, pile them up, and warm themselves with them. During the winter they are sold, like lumps of peat. And what do you suppose the best paid dressmaker earns? Five sous a day,' she said, after a pause; 'but she gets her board.'

'See,' I said to her, 'the winds from the ocean wither or uproot everything; there are no trees; the wrecks of vessels that are beyond use are sold to the rich, for the cost of transportation prevents them from using the firewood in which Brittany abounds. This province is beautiful only to great souls; people without courage could not live here; it is no place for anybody except poets or barnacles. The storehouse for salt had to be built on the cliff, to induce anybody to live in it. On one side, the sea; on the other, the sands; above, space.'

We had already passed the town and were within the species of desert which separates Le Croisic from the village of Batz. Imagine, my dear uncle, a plain two leagues in length, covered by the gleaming sand that we see on the seashore. Here and there a few rocks raised their heads, and you would have said that they were gigantic beasts lying among the dunes. Along the shore there is an occasional reef, about which the waves play, giving them the aspect of great white roses floating on the liquid expanse and coming to rest on the shore. When I saw that plain bounded by the ocean on the right, and on the left by the great lake that flows in between Le Croisic and the sandy heights of Guérande, at the foot of which there are salt marshes absolutely without vegetation, I glanced at Pauline and asked her if she had the courage to defy the heat of the sun, and the strength to walk through the sand.

'I have on high boots; let us go thither,' she said, pointing to the tower of Batz, which circumscribed the view by its enormous mass, placed there like a pyramid, but a slender, indented pyramid, so poetically adorned that it allowed the imagination to see in it the first ruins of a great Asiatic city. We walked a few yards and sat down under a rock which was still in the shadow; but it was eleven o'clock in the morning, and that shadow, which ceased at our feet, rapidly disappeared.

'How beautiful the silence is,' she said to me; 'and how its intensity is increased by the regular plashing of the sea on the beach!'

'If you choose to abandon your understanding to the three immensities that surround us, the air, the water, and the sand, listening solely to the repeated sound of the flow and the outflow,' I replied, 'you will not be able to endure its language; you will fancy that you discover therein a thought which will overwhelm you. Yesterday, at sunset, I had that sensation; it prostrated me.'

'Oh, yes, let us talk,' she said, after a long pause. 'No orator can be more terrible than this silence. I fancy that I have discovered the causes of the harmony which surrounds us,' she continued. 'This landscape, which has only three sharp colours, the brilliant yellow of the sand, the blue of the sky, and the smooth green of the sea, is grand without being wild, it is immense without being a desert, it is changeless without being monotonous; it has only three elements, but it is diversified.'

'Women alone can express their impressions thus,' I replied; 'you would drive a poet to despair, dear heart, whom I divined so perfectly.'

'The excessive noonday heat imparts a gorgeous colour to those three expressions of infinity,' replied Pauline, laughing. 'I can imagine here the poesy and the passion of the Orient.'

'And I can imagine its despair.'

'Yes,' she said; 'that dune is a sublime cloister.'

We heard the hurried step of our guide; he had dressed himself in his best clothes. We said a few formal words to him; he evidently saw that our frame of mind had changed, and, with the reserve that misfortune imparts, he kept silent. Although we pressed each other's hands from time to time, to advise each other of the unity of our impressions, we walked for half an hour in silence, whether because we were overwhelmed by the heat, which rose in shimmering waves from the sand, or because the difficulty of walking absorbed our attention. We walked on, hand in hand, like two children; we should not have taken a dozen steps if we had been arm in arm. The road leading to Batz was not marked out; a gust of wind was enough to efface the footprints of horses or the wheel-ruts; but our guide's practised eye recognised the road by the droppings of cattle or of horses. Sometimes it went down towards the sea, sometimes rose towards the upland, at the caprice of the slopes, or to skirt a rock. At noon we were only half-way.

'We will rest there,' said I, pointing to a promontory formed of rocks high enough to lead one to suppose that we should find a grotto there.

When I spoke, the fisherman, who had followed the direction of my finger, shook his head and said:

'There's some one there! People who go from Batz to Le Croisic, or from Le Croisic to Batz, always make a détour in order not to pass that rock.'

The man said this in a low voice, and we divined a mystery.

'Is he a thief, an assassin?'

Our guide replied only by a long-drawn breath which increased our curiosity.

'But will anything happen to us if we pass by there?'

'Oh no!'

'Will you go with us?'

'No, monsieur.'

'We will go then, if you assure us that we shall be in no danger.'

'I don't say that,' replied the fisherman hastily; 'I say simply that the man who is there won't say anything to you, or do any harm to you. Oh, bless my soul! he won't so much as move from his place!'

'Who is he, pray?'

'A man!'

Never were two syllables uttered in such a tragic tone. At that moment we were twenty yards from that reef, about which the sea was playing; our guide took the road which skirted the rocks; we went straight ahead, but Pauline took my arm. Our guide quickened his pace in order to reach the spot where the two roads met again at the same time that we did. He evidently supposed that, after seeing the man, we would quicken our pace. That circumstance kindled our curiosity, which then became so intense that our hearts throbbed as if they had felt a thrill of fear. Despite the heat of the day and the fatigue caused by walking through the sand, our hearts were still abandoned to the indescribable languor of a blissful harmony of sensations; they were filled with that pure pleasure which can only be described by comparing it to the pleasure which one feels in listening to some lovely music, like Mozart's *Andiano mio ben*. Do not two pure sentiments, which blend, resemble two beautiful voices, singing? In order fully to appreciate the emotion which seized us, you must share the semi-voluptuous condition in which the events of that morning had enveloped us. Gaze for a long while at a turtle-dove perched on a slender twig, near a spring, and you will utter a cry of pain when you see a hawk pounce upon it, bury its steel claws in its heart, and bear it away with the murderous rapidity that power communicates to the bullet.

When we had walked a yard or two across the open space that lay in front of the grotto, a sort of platform a hundred feet above the ocean, and sheltered from its rage by a succession of steep rocks, we were conscious of an electric shock not unlike that caused by a sudden noise in the midst of the night. We had spied a man seated on a boulder of granite, and he had looked at us. His glance, like the flash of a cannon, came from two bloodshot eyes, and his stoical immobility could be compared only to the unchanging posture of the masses of granite which surrounded him. His eyes moved slowly; his body, as if it were petrified, did not move at all. After flashing at us that glance which gave us such a rude shock, he turned his eyes to the vast expanse of the ocean, and gazed at it, despite the dazzling light which rose therefrom, as the eagles are said to gaze at the sun, without lowering the lids, which he did not raise again. Try to recall, my dear uncle, one of those old druidical oaks, whose gnarled trunk, newly stripped of its branches, rises fantastically above a deserted road, and you will have an accurate image of that man. He had one of those shattered herculean frames, and the face of Olympian Jove, but ravaged by age, by the hard toil of the seafaring man, by grief, by coarse food, and blackened as if struck by lightning. As I glanced at his calloused, hairy hands, I saw chords which resembled veins of iron. However, everything about him indicated a robust constitution. I noticed a large quantity of moss in a corner of the grotto, and upon a rough table, hewn out by chance in the midst of the granite, a broken loaf covering an earthen jug. Never had my imagination, when it carried me back to the deserts where the first hermits of Christianity lived, conceived a face more grandly religious or more appallingly penitent than was the face of that man.

Even you, who have listened to confessions, my dear uncle, have perhaps never met with such sublime remorse; but that remorse was drowned in the waves of prayer, the incessant prayer of silent despair. That fisherman, that sailor, that rude Breton, was sublime by virtue of some unknown sentiment. But had those eyes wept? Had that statue-like hand struck its fellow-man? Was that stern forehead, instinct with pitiless uprightness, on which, however, strength had left those marks of gentleness which are the accompaniment of all true strength – was that forehead, furrowed by wrinkles, in harmony with a noble heart? Why was that man among the granite? Why the granite in that man? Where was the man? Where was the granite? A whole world of thoughts rushed through our minds. As our guide had anticipated, we had passed in silence, rapidly; and when he met us, we were tremulous with terror, or overwhelmed with amazement. But he did not use the fulfilment of his prediction as a weapon against us.

'Did you see him?' he asked.

'Who is that man?' said I.

'They call him *The Man of the Vow*.'

You can imagine how quickly our two faces turned toward our fisherman at those words! He was a simple-minded man; he understood our silent question; and this is what he said, in his own language, the popular tone of which I shall try to retain:

'Madame, the people of Le Croisic, like the people of Batz, believe that that man is guilty of something, and that he is doing a penance ordered by a famous priest to whom he went to confess, a long way beyond Nantes. Other people think that Cambremer – that's his name – has an evil spell that he communicates to everybody who passes through the air he breathes. So a good many people, before they pass that rock, look to see what way the wind is. If it's from *galerne*,' he said, pointing towards the west, 'they wouldn't go on, even if it was a matter of searching for a piece of the true Cross; they turn back, because they're frightened. Other people, the rich people of Le Croisic, say that he's made a vow, and that's why he's called *The Man of the Vow*. He is always there, night and day; never comes out.

'These reports about him have some appearance of sense. You see,' he added, turning to point out a thing which we had not noticed, 'he has stuck up there, on the left, a wooden cross, to show that he has put himself under the protection of God, the Blessed Virgin, and the saints. Even if he hadn't consecrated himself like that, the fear everybody has of him would make him as safe there as if he were guarded by soldiers. He hasn't said a word since he shut himself up there in the open air; he lives on bread and water that his brother's daughter brings him every morning – a little maid of twelve years, that he's left his property to; and she's a pretty thing, as gentle as a lamb, a nice little girl and very clever. She has blue eyes as long as that,' he said, holding up his thumb, 'and a cherub's head of hair.

'When any one says to her: "I say, Pérotte" (that means Pierrette amongst us,' he said, interrupting himself: 'she is consecrated to St. Pierre; Cambremer's name is Pierre, and he was her godfather), "I say, Pérotte, what does your uncle say to you?" "He don't say anything," she'll answer, "not anything at all, nothing!" "Well, then, what does he do to you?" "He kisses me on the forehead Sundays!" "Aren't you afraid of him?" "Why no, he's my godfather." He won't let anyone else bring him anything to eat. Pérotte says that he smiles when she comes; but that's like a sunbeam in a fog, for they say he's as gloomy as a fog.'

'But,' I said, 'you arouse our curiosity without gratifying it. Do you know what brought him here? Was it grief, was it repentance, was it insanity, was it crime, was it —?'

'Oh! only my father and I know the truth of the thing, monsieur. My dead mother worked for a judge to whom Cambremer told the whole story, by the priest's order; for he wouldn't give him absolution on any other condition, according to what the people at the harbour said. My poor mother overheard what Cambremer said, without meaning to, because the judge's kitchen was right next to his study, and she listened. She's dead, and the judge who heard him is dead. My mother made father and me promise never to tell anything to the people about here; but I can tell you that the night my mother told it to us, the hair on my head turned grey.'

'Well, tell us, my fine fellow; we will not mention it to anybody.'

The fisherman looked at us, and continued thus:

'Pierre Cambremer, whom you saw yonder, is the oldest of the Cambremers, who have always been sailors, from father to son; that's what their name says – the sea has always bent under them. The man you saw was a boat fisherman. So he had boats and went sardine-fishing; he went deep-sea fishing, too, for the dealers. He'd have fitted out a vessel and gone after cod, if he hadn't been so fond of his wife; a fine woman she was, a Brouin from Guérande; a magnificent girl, and she had a big heart. She was so fond of Cambremer that she'd never let her man leave her any longer than he had to, to go after sardines. They used to live over there – look!' said the fisherman, ascending a hillock to point to an islet in the little inland sea between the dunes, across which we were walking, and the salt marshes of Guérande. 'Do you see that house? That was his.

'Jacquette Brouin and Cambremer never had but one child, a boy; and they loved him like – like what shall I say? – indeed, like people love their only child; they were mad over him. If their little Jacques had put dirt in the saucepan, saving your presence, they'd have thought it was sugar. How many times we've seen 'em at the fair, buying the prettiest fallals for him! It was all nonsense – everybody told 'em so. Little Cambremer, seeing that he was allowed to do whatever he wanted to, became as big a rogue as a red ass.

'When any one went to the elder Cambremer and told him: "Your boy nearly killed little So-and-so," he'd laugh and say: "Bah! he'll make a fine sailor! he'll command the king's fleet." And when somebody else said: "Pierre Cambremer, do you know that your boy put out the little Pougaud girl's eye?" Pierre said: "He'll be fond of the girls!" He thought everything was all right. So my little scamp, when he was ten years old,

used to be at everybody, and amuse himself cutting off hens'
heads, cutting pigs open; in short, he rolled in blood like a
polecat. "He'll make a famous soldier!" Cambremer would
say; "he's got a taste for blood." I remember all that, you see,'
said the fisherman.

'And so did Cambremer too,' he continued after a pause.
'When he got to be fifteen or sixteen years old, Jacques
Cambremer was – what shall I say? – a shark. He used to go to
Guérande to enjoy himself, or to Savenay to make love to the
girls. Then he began to steal from his mother, who didn't dare
to say anything to her husband. Cambremer was so honest
that he'd travel twenty leagues to pay back two sous, if he had
been overpaid in settling an account. At last the day came
when his mother was stripped clean. While his father was
away fishing, the boy carried off the sideboard, the dishes, the
sheets, the linen, and left just the four walls; he'd sold
everything to get money to go to Nantes and raise the devil.
The poor woman cried for whole days and nights. She
couldn't help telling the father about that, when he came
home; and she was afraid of the father – not for herself, oh no!
When Pierre Cambremer came home and found his house
furnished with things people had lent his wife, he said:

'"What does all this mean?"

'The poor woman was nearer dead than alive.

'"We've been robbed," said she.

'"Where's Jacques?"

'"Jacques is on a spree."

'No one knew where the villain had gone.

'"He goes on too many sprees!" said Pierre.

'Six months later, the poor man learned that his son was in
danger of falling into the hands of justice at Nantes. He went
there on foot; made the journey faster than he could have gone
by sea, got hold of his son, and brought him back here. He
didn't ask him: "What have you been doing?" He just said to
him:

'"If you don't behave yourself here with your mother and
me for two years, going fishing and acting like an honest man,
you'll have an account to settle with me!"

'The idiot, counting on his father's and mother's stupidity,
made a face at him. At that Pierre fetched him a crack that laid

Master Jacques up in bed for six months. The poor mother almost died of grief. One night, when she was sleeping peacefully by her husband's side, she heard a noise, got out of bed, and got a knife-cut on her arm. She shrieked and some one brought a light. Pierre Cambremer found his wife wounded; he thought that a robber did it – as if there was any such thing in our province, where you can carry ten thousand francs in gold from Le Croisic to St.-Nazaire, without fear, and without once being asked what you've got under your arm! Pierre looked for Jacques, but couldn't find him.

'In the morning, the little monster had the face to come home and say that he'd been to Batz. I must tell you that his mother didn't know where to hide her money. Cambremer always left his with Monsieur Dupotet at Le Croisic. Their son's wild ways had eaten up crowns by the hundred, francs by the hundred, and louis d'or; they were almost ruined, and that was pretty hard for folks who used to have about twelve thousand francs, including their island. No one knew what Cambremer paid out at Nantes to clear his son. Bad luck raised the deuce with the family. Cambremer's brother was in a bad way and needed help. To encourage him, Pierre told him that Jacques and Pérotte (the younger Cambremer's daughter) should marry.

'Then he employed him in the fishing, so that he could earn his living; for Joseph Cambremer was reduced to living by his work. His wife had died of a fever, and he had had to pay for a wet-nurse for Pérotte. Pierre Cambremer's wife owed a hundred francs to different people on the little girl's account, for linen and clothes, and for two or three months' wages for that big Frelu girl, who had a child by Simon Gaudry, and who nursed Pérotte. Mère Cambremer had sewed a Spanish coin into the cover of her mattress, and marked it: "For Pérotte." She had had a good education; she could write like a clerk, and she'd taught her son to read; that was the ruin of him. No one knew how it happened, but that scamp of a Jacques scented the gold, stole it, and went off to Le Croisic on a spree.

'As luck would have it, Goodman Cambremer came in with his boat. As he approached the beach, he saw a piece of paper floating; he picked it up and took it in to his wife, who fell flat

when she recognised her own written words. Cambremer
didn't say anything, but he went to Le Croisic, and found out
that his son was playing billiards; then he sent for the good
woman who keeps the café, and said:

'"I told Jacques not to spend a gold-piece that he'll pay you
with; I'll wait outside; you bring it to me, and I'll give you
silver for it."

'The good woman brought him the money. Cambremer
took it, said: "All right!" and went home. The whole town
heard about that. But here's something that I know, and that
other people only suspect in a general way. He told his wife to
clean up their room, which was on the ground floor; he made
a fire on the hearth, lighted two candles, placed two chairs on
one side of the fireplace and a stool on the other. Then he told
his wife to put out his wedding clothes and to get into her
own. When he was dressed, he went to his brother and told
him to watch in front of the house and tell him if he heard any
noise on either of the beaches, this one or the one in front of
the Guérande salt marshes. When he thought that his wife was
dressed, he went home again, loaded a gun, and put it out of
sight in the corner of the fireplace. Jacques came at last; it was
late; he had been drinking and playing billiards till ten o'clock;
he had come home by the point of Carnouf. His uncle heard
him hailing, crossed to the beach in front of the marsh to fetch
him, and rowed him to the island without a word. When he
went into the house, his father said to him:

'"Sit down there," pointing to the stool. "You are before
your father and mother, whom you have outraged, and who
have got to try you."

'Jacques began to bellow, because Cambremer's face was
working in a strange way. The mother sat as stiff as an oar.

'"If you call out, if you move, if you don't sit on your stool
as straight as a mast, I'll shoot you like a dog," said Pierre,
pointing his gun at him.

'The son was dumb as a fish; the mother didn't say
anything.

'"Here," said Pierre to his son, "is a paper that was wrapped
round a Spanish gold-piece; the gold-piece was in your
mother's bed; nobody else knew where she had put it; I found
the paper on the water as I was coming ashore; you gave this

Spanish gold-piece to Mother Fleurant tonight, and your mother can't find hers in her bed. Explain yourself!"

'Jacques said that he didn't take the money from his mother, and that he had had the coin ever since he went to Nantes.

'"So much the better," said Pierre. "How can you prove it?"

'"I had it before."

'"You didn't take your mother's?"

'"No."

'"Will you swear it by your everlasting life?"

'He was going to swear; his mother looked up at him and said:

'"Jacques, my child, be careful; don't swear, if it isn't true. You may mend your ways and repent; there's time enough still."

'And she began to cry.

'"You're neither one thing nor the other," he said, "and you've always wanted to ruin me."

'Cambremer turned pale, and said:

'"What you just said to your mother will lengthen your account. Come to the point! Will you swear?"

'"Yes."

'"See," said Pierre, "did your piece have this cross which the sardine-dealer who paid it to me had made on ours?"

'Jacques sobered off, and began to cry.

'"Enough talk," said Pierre. "I don't say anything about what you've done before this. I don't propose that a Cambremer shall be put to death on the public square at Le Croisic. Say your prayers, and make haste! A priest is coming to confess you."

'The mother went out, so that she needn't hear her son's sentence. When she had left the room, Cambremer the uncle arrived with the rector of Piriac; but Jacques wouldn't say anything to him. He was sly; he knew his father well enough to be sure that he wouldn't kill him without confession.

'"Thank you, monsieur; excuse us," said Cambremer to the priest, when he saw that Jacques was obstinate. "I meant to give my son a lesson, and I ask you not to say anything about it. – If you don't mend your ways," he said to Jacques, "the next time will be the last, and I'll put an end to it without confession."

'He sent him off to bed. The boy believed what he had heard, and imagined that he could arrange matters with his father. He went to sleep. The father sat up. When he saw that his son was sound asleep, he stuffed his mouth with hemp and tied a strip of canvas over it very tight; then he bound his hands and feet. Jacques stormed and wept blood, so Cambremer told the judge. What could you expect! The mother threw herself at the father's feet.

'"He has been tried," he said; "you must help me put him in the boat."

'She refused. Cambremer took him to the boat all alone, laid him in the bottom, tied a stone round his neck, and rowed abreast of the rock where he is now. Then the poor mother, who had got her brother-in-law to bring her over here, cried: "Mercy!" All in vain; it had the effect of a stone thrown at a wolf. The moon was shining; she saw the father throw their son into the water, the son to whom her heart still clung; and as there wasn't any wind, she heard a splash, then nothing more, not a sound or a bubble; the sea's a famous keeper, I tell you! When he came ashore here to quiet his wife, who was groaning, Cambremer found her about the same as dead. The two brothers couldn't carry her, so they had to put her in the boat that had just held the son, and they took her home, going round through Le Croisic passage. Ah! *La Belle Brouin*, as they called her, didn't last a week. She died asking her husband to burn the accursed boat. He did it, too. As for him, he was like a crazy man; he didn't know what he wanted, and he staggered when he walked, like a man who can't carry his wine. Then he went off for ten days, and when he came back he planted himself where you saw him, and since he's been there he hasn't said a word.'

The fisherman took only a moment or two in telling us this story, and he told it even more simply than I have written it. The common people make few comments when they tell a story; they select the point that has made an impression on them, and interpret it as they feel it. That narrative was as sharp and incisive as a blow with an axe.

'I shall not go to Batz,' said Pauline, as we reached the upper end of the lake.

We returned to Le Croisic by way of the salt marshes, guided through their labyrinth by a fisherman who had become as silent as we. The current of our thoughts had changed. We were both absorbed by depressing reflections, saddened by that drama which explained the swift presentiment that we had felt at the sight of Cambremer. We both had sufficient knowledge of the world to divine all that our guide had not told us of that triple life. The misfortunes of those three people were reproduced before us as if we had seen them in the successive scenes of a drama, to which that father, by thus expiating his necessary crime, had added the dénouement. We dared not look back at that fatal man who terrified a whole province.

A few clouds darkened the sky; vapours were rising along the horizon. We were walking through the most distressingly desolate tract of land that I have ever seen; the very soil beneath our feet seemed sickly and suffering – salt marshes, which may justly be termed the scrofula of the earth. There the ground is divided into parcels of unequal size, all enclosed by enormous heaps of grey earth, and filled with brackish water, to the surface of which the salt rises. These ravines, made by the hand of man, are subdivided by causeways along which workmen walk, armed with long rakes, with which they skim off the brine, and carry the salt to round platforms built here and there, when it is in condition to pile. For two hours we skirted that dismal chess-board, where the salt is so abundant that it chokes the vegetation, and where we saw no other living beings than an occasional *paludier* – the name given to the men who gather the salt.

These men, or rather this tribe of Bretons, wear a special costume: a white jacket not unlike that worn by brewers. They intermarry, and there has never been an instance of a girl of that tribe marrying anybody except a *paludier*. The ghastly aspect of those swamps, where the surface of the mire is neatly raked, and of that greyish soil, which the Breton flora hold in horror, harmonised with the mourning of our hearts. When we reached the place where we were to cross the arm of the sea which is formed by the eruption of the water into that basin, and which serves doubtless to supply the salt marshes with their staple, we rejoiced to see the meagre vegetation scattered along the sandy shore. As we crossed, we saw, in the centre of the lake, the islet where the Cambremers lived; we looked the other way.

When we reached our hotel, we noticed a billiard-table in a room on the ground floor; and, when we learned that it was the only public billiard-table in Le Croisic, we prepared for our departure that night. The next day we were at Guérande. Pauline was still depressed, and I could already feel the coming of the flame that is consuming my brain. I was so cruelly tormented by my visions of those three lives that she said to me:

'Write the story, Louis; in that way you will change the nature of this fever.'

So I have written it down for you, my dear uncle; but it has already destroyed the tranquillity that I owed to the sea-baths and to our visit here.

FACINO CANE

FACINO CANE

I was living in a small street of which doubtless you do not
even know the name, the Rue des Lesdiguières. It begins at the
Rue St. Antoine opposite the fountain near the Place de la
Bastille, and runs into the Rue de la Cerisaie. The love of
learning had flung me into a garret where I worked during the
night, and I passed the day in a neighbouring library, the
Bibliothèque de Monsieur. I lived frugally. I had accepted all
those conditions of a monastic life that are so necessary to
workers. When it was fine I barely allowed myself a walk on
the Boulevard Bourdon. One passion only drew me away
from my studious habits, but was not even that a sort of
study? I would go out to observe the manners of the
Faubourg, its inhabitants and their characters.

As badly dressed as the workmen themselves and careless
about keeping up an appearance, I did not make them in any
way suspicious of me. I could mingle freely with them, and
watch them making their bargains and quarrelling amongst
themselves as they left their work. With me the power of
observation had already become intuitive. It penetrated to the
soul, without leaving the body out of account: or rather, it
grasped so well the outer details, that it went at once beyond
them; it gave me the power of living the life of the individual
on whom I brought it to bear, thus permitting me in fancy to
substitute myself for him, as the dervish in the *Arabian Nights*
took the body and soul of the persons over whom he
pronounced certain words.

When between eleven o'clock and midnight I met a workman and his wife returning together from the Ambigu
Comique, I amused myself by following them from the
Boulevard du Pont-aux-Choux as far as the Boulevard
Beaumarchais. These good people would talk at first of the
piece they had just seen. From one thing to another they
would get on to their own affairs. The mother would be

dragging her child by the hand without heeding either its complaints or its questions. The pair would reckon up the money that would be paid them next day, and spend it in twenty different ways. Then came household details; complaints as to the excessive price of potatoes, or about the length of the winter and the dearness of peat fuel; strong representations as to the amount owing to the baker; and at last disputes that became a bit angry, and in which the character of each came out in picturesque expressions.

While listening to these people I could enter into their life; I felt myself with their rags on my back; I walked with my feet in their broken shoes; their desires, their needs all came into my soul, or my soul passed into theirs. It was the dream of one who was still wide awake. With them I grew angry against the foremen of the workshops who tyrannised over them, or against the bad custom that forced them to come again and again to ask in vain for their pay. To get away from my ordinary occupations, to become some one else by this over excitation of my mental faculties, and to play this game at my will – this was my recreation. To what do I owe this gift? Is it a kind of second sight? or is it one of those powers the abuse of which would lead to insanity? I have never investigated the sources of this faculty of mine; I possess it and I make use of it, that is all.

I need only tell you that in those days I had analysed the elements of that heterogeneous mass called 'the people,' so that I could estimate their good and bad qualities. Already I knew all that was to be learned from that famous Faubourg, that nursery of Revolutions, which gives shelter at once to heroes, inventors, and practical scientists, and knaves and scoundrels, – to virtues and vices, all huddled together by misery, stifled by poverty, drowned in wine, wasted by strong drink. You would never imagine how many unknown adventures, how many forgotten dramas belong to that city of sorrow. How many horrible and beautiful things! For imagination would never go so far as the reality that is hidden there, and that no one can go there and discover. One has to go down to too great a depth if one is to find out those wonderful scenes of living tragedy or comedy, masterpieces that chance has brought into being.

I know not why I have so long kept untold the story that I am going to relate to you; it is one of those strange tales that are laid by in the bag from which memory draws them out haphazard like the numbers of a lottery. I have plenty of others quite as singular as this one, buried away in the same fashion; but they will have their turn, believe me.

One day my housekeeper, a working-man's wife, came and asked me to honour with my presence the wedding of one of her sisters. In order to enable you to understand what sort of a wedding it would be I must tell you that I used to pay forty sous a month to this poor creature, who came in every morning to make my bed, polish my shoes, brush my clothes, sweep the room, and get my breakfast ready. For the rest of her time she went to turn the handle of a mangle, and by this hard work earned ten sous a day. Her husband, a cabinet-maker, earned four francs.

But, as their household included three children, they could barely pay for the bread they ate. I have never come across more real respectability than that of this man and wife. Five years after I had left the neighbourhood Dame Vaillant came to wish me a happy name day, and brought me a bunch of flowers and some oranges as presents – she who had never been in a position to save ten sous. Poverty had drawn us together. I was never able to pay her more than ten francs, often borrowed for the occasion. This will explain my promise to go to the wedding; I counted on taking an unobtrusive part in the rejoicings of these poor people.

The feast and the dance were both held at a wine shop in the Rue de Charenton, in a large room on the first storey. It was lighted with lamps with tin reflectors; the paper showed grease spots at the level of the tables, and along the walls there were wooden benches. In this room some eighty people, dressed in their Sunday clothes, decked out with flowers and ribbons, all full of the holiday spirit, danced with flushed faces as if the world was coming to an end. The happy pair kissed each other amid a general outbreak of satisfaction, and one heard 'Eh! eh!' and 'Ah! ah!' pronounced in a tone of amusement, that all the same was more respectable than the timid ogling of young women of a better class. Every one manifested a rough and ready pleasure that had in it something infectious.

But neither the general aspect of the gathering, nor the wedding, nor anything of the kind, has really to do with our story. Only I want you to keep in mind the quaint setting of it all. Imagine to yourself the shabby shop, with its decorations of red paint, smell the odour of the wine, listen to the shouts of delight, keep to the Faubourg, in the midst of these workers, these old men, these poor women abandoning themselves to one night of pleasure.

The orchestra was made up of three blind men from the Hospice des Quinze-Vingts; the first was the violin, the second the clarionet, and the third the flageolet. All three were paid one lump sum of seven francs for the night. At this price, of course, they gave us neither Rossini nor Beethoven; they played what they liked and what they could, and with a charming delicacy of feeling no one found fault with them for it! Their music was such a rough trial to my ears, that, after a glance at the audience, I looked at the trio of blind men, and recognising the uniform of the hospice, I felt from the first disposed to be indulgent. These artists were seated in the deep bay of a window, and thus in order to be able to distinguish their features one had to be near them.

I did not at once come close to them; but when I approached them I cannot say how it was, but all was over with me, I forgot the marriage and the music; my curiosity was excited to the highest pitch, for my soul passed into the body of the clarionet player. The violin and the flageolet had both commonplace features, the well-known face of the blind, with its strained look, all attention and seriousness; but that of the clarionet player was one of those phenomenal faces that make the artist or the philosopher stop at once to look at them.

Imagine a plaster mask of Dante, lighted up with the red glare of an Argand-lamp, and crowned with a forest of silver-white hair. His blindness added to the bitter sorrowful expression of this splendid face, for one could imagine the dead eyes were alive again; a burning light seemed to shine out from them, the expression of a single ceaseless desire that had set its deep marks on the rounded forehead, which was scored by wrinkles like the lines of an old wall. The old man was blowing away at haphazard, without paying the least attention to time or tune, his fingers rising and falling, and moving the old keys through mere mechanical habit. He did not trouble about making what is called in the slang of the orchestra 'quacks,' and the dancers took no more notice of this than the two comrades of my Italian did – for I made up my mind that he must be an Italian, and an Italian he was. There was something noble and commanding to be seen in this aged Homer, who kept all to himself some Odyssey destined to forgetfulness. It was a nobility so real that it still triumphed over his obscurity; an air of command so striking that it rose superior to his poverty.

None of the strong feelings that lead a man to good as well as to evil, that make of him a convict or a hero, were wanting to this splendidly outlined face, with its sallow Italian complexion, and the shadows of the iron-grey eyebrows that threw their shade over the deep cavities in which one would tremble at seeing the light of thought appear once more, as one fears to see brigands armed with torch and dagger show themselves at the mouth of a cavern. There was a lion in that cage of flesh, a lion of which the fury had uselessly spent itself on the iron of its bars. The fire of despair had burned out among its ashes, the lava had cooled; but rifts, fallen rocks, and a little smoke told of the violence of the eruption, the ravages of the fire. These ideas called up by the aspect of the man were as warmly pictured in my mind, as they were coldly marked upon his face.

In the interval between each dance the violin and the flageolet, becoming seriously occupied with a bottle and glasses, hung their instruments to a button of their reddish tunics, and stretched out a hand to a little table standing in the bay of the window, on which were their refreshments. They always offered the Italian a full glass, which he could not have got unaided, for the table was behind his chair. Each time the clarionet thanked them with a friendly nod of his head. Their movements were carried out with that precision which always seems so astonishing in the case of the blind folk from the Quinze-Vingts, and which seems to make one think they can see. I drew near to the three blind men to listen to them, but when I stood near them they somehow scrutinised me, and doubtless failing to recognise the workman type in me, they said not a word.

'From what country are you, you who play the clarionet?'

'From Venice,' answered the blind man, with a slight Italian accent.

'Were you born blind, or were you blinded by . . .'

'By a mishap,' he replied sharply; 'a cursed amaurosis in my eyes.'

'Venice is a beautiful city. I have always had an idea of going there.'

The face of the old man became animated, its furrows rose and fell, he was strongly moved.

'If I went there with you, you would not lose your time,' said he to me.

'Don't talk of Venice to him,' said the violin to me, 'or our Doge will start his story. Besides that he has already two bottles under his belt, the old prince!'

'Come, let us be getting on, Père Canard,' said the flageolet.

All three began to play; but all the time that they were going through the four parts of the quadrille the Venetian was sizing me up; he guessed the extraordinary interest I took in him. His face lost its cold expression of sadness. Some hope or other brightened all his features – played like a blue flame in the wrinkles of his face. He smiled as he wiped his forehead – that forehead with its bold and terrible look; finally he became quite gay, like a man who is getting up on his hobby.

'What is your age?' I asked him.

'Eighty-two years.'

'How long have you been blind?'

'It will soon be fifty years,' he replied, in a tone which suggested that his regret was not only for the loss of his sight, but also for some great power of which he had been deprived.

'But why do they call you the Doge?' I asked him.

'Ah! that's a joke,' he said; 'I am a patrician of Venice, and I could have been a Doge as well as any one else.'

'What is your name them?'

'Here,' he said, 'I am old Canet. My name has never appeared otherwise on the local registers. But in Italian it is Marco Facino Cane, Prince of Varese.'

'What! Are you descended from the famous condottiere, Facino Cane, whose conquests passed into the possession of the Dukes of Milan?'

'*É vero* (that's true),' said he. 'In those times the son of Cane, to escape being killed by the Visconti, took refuge in Venice, and had his name inscribed in the Golden Book of nobility. But now neither the Book nor any of the House of Cane is left!'

And he made a startling gesture to signify his feeling that patriotism was dead, and his disgust for human affairs.

'But if you were a Senator of Venice, you must have been rich. How did you come to lose your fortune?'

At this question he raised his head, turning to me as if regarding me with a movement full of truest tragedy, and replied to me:

'In the midst of mis-fortunes!'

He no longer thought of drinking; with a wave of his hand he refused the glass of wine which the old flageolet player offered him at this moment, then he bowed down his head.

These details were not of a kind to put an end to my curiosity. During the quadrille that the three instruments played in mechanical style, I watched the old Venetian noble with the feelings that devour a man of only twenty. I saw Venice and the Adriatic, and I saw its ruin in this ruined face. I was moving about in that city so beloved of its inhabitants. I went from the Rialto to the Grand Canal, from the Riva degli Schiavoni to the Lido; I came back to its cathedral so sublime in its originality; I looked up at the windows of the Casa d'Oro, each of which has different ornaments; I contemplated its old palaces so rich in marbles – in a word, all those wonders that move the student's feelings all the more when he can colour them with his fancy, and does not spoil the poetry of his dreams by the sight of the reality.

I traced backward the course of the life of this scion of the greatest of the condottieri, seeking out in it the traces of his misfortunes and the causes of the deep physical and moral degradation that made the sparks of greatness and nobility that shone again at that moment seem all the finer. Our thoughts were no doubt in mutual accord, for I believe that blindness makes mental communication much more rapid, by preventing the attention from dispersing itself on external things. I had not long to wait for a proof of our bond of feeling. Facino Cane stopped playing, rose, came to me and

said, 'Come out,' in a way that produced on me the effect of
an electric shock. I gave him my arm and we went away.

When we were in the street, he said to me:

'Will you take me to Venice, guide me there? Will you have
confidence in me? You will be richer than the ten richest firms
of Amsterdam or London; richer than the Rothschilds; in a
word, rich as the *Arabian Nights*.'

I thought the man was mad. But there was in his voice a
power that I obeyed. I let him lead me, and he took me in the
direction of the ditches of the Bastille, as if he still had the use
of his eyes. He sat down on a stone in a very lonely place,
where, since then, the bridge has been built under which the
Canal Saint Martin passes to the Seine. I took my place on
another stone facing the old man, whose white hairs glittered
like threads of silver in the moonlight. The silence, hardly
disturbed by such stormy sounds as reached us from the
Boulevards, the brightness of the night, all helped to make the
scene something fantastic.

'You talk of millions to a young man, and you think that he
would hesitate to endure a thousand ills to secure them! Are
you not making a jest of me?'

'May I die without confession,' said he fiercely, 'if what I
am about to tell you is not true! I was once a young man of
twenty as you are now. I was rich. I was handsome. I was
noble. I began with the first of all follies – love. I loved as men
no longer love, going so far as to hide in a chest at the risk of
being stabbed, without having received anything else but the
promise of a kiss. To die for her seemed to me worth a whole
life. In 1760 I fell in love with one of the Vendramini, a girl of
eighteen, married to a certain Sagredo, one of the richest of the
Senators, a man of thirty years, madly devoted to his wife.
My love and I, we were as innocent as two little cherubs when
the husband surprised us talking love together. I was
unarmed; he was armed, but he missed me. I sprang on him, I
strangled him with my two hands, twisting his neck like a
chicken's. I wanted to go away with Bianca, but she would
not go with me. That's what women are like! I went away
alone. I was condemned in my absence, my property was
confiscated for the benefit of my heirs; but I had carried off
with me my diamonds, five pictures by Titian rolled up, and

all my gold. I went to Milan, where I was not molested, for my affair did not interest the State.

'One little remark before going on,' he said, after a pause. 'Whether it is true or not that a woman's fancies influence her child before its birth, it is certain that my mother had a passion for gold while she was expecting mine. I have a monomania for gold, the satisfaction of which is so necessary for my very life, that in whatever circumstances I have been, I have never been without some gold in my possession. I am always handling gold. When I was young I always wore jewels, and I always carried about with me two or three hundred ducats'.

As he said these words he took two ducats out of his pocket and showed them to me.

'I can smell gold. Although I am blind, I stop in front of the jewellers' shops. This passion was my ruin. I became a gambler, to have the enjoyment of gold. I was not a swindler; I was swindled. I ruined myself. When I had no longer any of my fortune left I was seized with a wild longing to see Bianca again. I returned secretly to Venice. I found her once more; I was happy for six months, hidden with her, supported by her. I had a delightful thought of thus living my life to the end. Her hand was sought by the Proveditore of the Republic. He guessed he had a rival; in Italy they can almost smell them; he spied on us, and surprised us together, the coward! You can imagine what a sharp fight there was. I did not kill him, but I wounded him seriously. That adventure broke off my happiness. Since that day I never found any one like Bianca. I have had many pleasures. I lived at the court of Louis XV in the midst of the most famous women, but nowhere did I find the characteristics, the graces, the love of my fair Venetian.

'The Proveditore had his followers. He called them. The palace was surrounded. I defended myself, hoping to die before the eyes of my dear Bianca, who helped me to kill the Proveditore. Formerly this woman had refused to share my flight; now, after six months of happiness, she was ready to die my death, and received several blows. Entangled in a big cloak that they threw over me, I was rolled in it, carried to a gondola and conveyed to the dungeons of the Pozzi. I was only twenty-two years old then, and I held so fast to the fragment of my broken sword, that to get it from me they would have had to cut off my wrist. By a strange chance, or rather inspired by a thought for the future, I hid this bit of steel in a corner, in case it might be of use to me. I was given medical care. None of my wounds was mortal. At twenty-two one can recover from anything. I was doomed to die by decapitation, but I pretended to be ill in order to gain time. I believed that I was in a dungeon next to the canal. My plan was to escape by making a hole through the wall and swimming across the canal at the risk of drowning myself.

'Here are some of the reasons on which I based my hopes:

'Whenever the jailer brought me my food I read, by the light he carried, inscriptions scrawled upon the walls, such as, "Towards the palace," "Towards the canal," "Towards the underground passage," and at last succeeded in making out a general plan of the place. There were some small difficulties about it, but they could be explained by the actual state of the Palace of the Doges, which is not completed. With the cleverness that the desire to regain one's liberty gives one, by feeling with my fingers the surface of a stone, I succeeded in deciphering an Arabic inscription, by which the writer of the words intimated to his successors that he had loosened two stones in the lowest course of masonry, and dug beyond them eleven feet of a tunnel. In order to continue his task it was necessary to spread over the floor of the dungeon itself the little bits of stone and mortar produced by the work of excavation.

'Even if my keepers or the inquisitors had not felt quite easy in their minds on account of the very structure of the building, which made only an external surveillance necessary, the arrangement of the Pozzi dungeons, into which one descends by a few steps, made it possible gradually to raise the level of the floor without its being noticed by the jailers. The immense amount of work he had done had proved to be superfluous, at least for the man who had undertaken it, for the fact that it had been left unfinished told of the death of the unknown prisoner. In order that his zeal might not be useless for ever, it was necessary that some future prisoner should know Arabic; but I had studied Eastern languages at the Armenian convent of Venice. A sentence written on the back of one of the stones told the fate of this unfortunate man, who had died the victim of his immense riches, which Venice had coveted, and of which she had taken possession. It took me a month to arrive at any result. Whilst I was at work, and during the intervals when I was overwhelmed with fatigue, I heard the sound of gold, I thought I could see gold before me, I was dazzled by diamonds! . . . Oh! just wait.

'One night, my piece of steel, now blunted, came upon wood. I sharpened my broken fragment of a sword and made a hole in the wood. In order to work I used to drag myself along like a serpent on my stomach, and I stripped so as to dig like a mole, with my hands out in front of me, stretched on the stones I had already burrowed through. In two days I was to appear before my judges, so during this night I meant to make a last effort. I cut through the wood, and my blade struck against nothing beyond it.

'Imagine my surprise when I put my eye to the hole! I had penetrated the wainscot of an underground room, in which a dim light allowed me to see a great heap of gold. The Doge and one of the Council of Ten were in this cellar. I heard their voices. From their talk I gathered that here was the secret hoard of the Republic, the gifts of the Doges, and the reserves of booty known as the "share of Venice," and levied on the produce of over-sea expeditions.

'I was saved!

'When next the jailer came, I proposed to him to assist me to escape, and to go away with me, taking off with us all that we could carry. There was no reason to hesitate, and he agreed. A ship was about to sail for the Levant. Every precaution was taken. Bianca lent her aid to the plans I dictated to my accomplice. In order not to arouse suspicion Bianca was to rejoin us only at Smyrna. In a single night the hole was enlarged, and we climbed down into the secret treasury of Venice. What a night! I saw four huge casks full of gold. In the room before that, silver was in the same profusion, piled up in two heaps, leaving a path in the middle by which to pass through the room, with the coins sloping up in piles on each side till they reached a height of five feet at the walls. I thought the jailer would go mad.

'He sang, he danced, he laughed, he cut capers among the gold. I threatened to strangle him if he wasted our time or

made a noise. In his joy he did not at first notice a table on
which were the diamonds. I threw myself upon it so cleverly
that I was able, unseen by him, to fill with them my sailor's
jacket and the pockets of my trousers. Mon Dieu! but I did not
take one-third of them. Under this table there were ingots of
gold. I persuaded my comrade to fill as many sacks as we
could carry with gold, pointing out to him that this was the
only way in which our plunder would not lead to our being
discovered abroad.

'"Pearls, jewels, and diamonds would only lead to our
being recognised," I said to him.

'Whatever might be our eagerness for it, we could not take
away more than two thousand pounds of gold, and this
required six journeys through the prison to get it to the
gondola. The sentinel at the water gate had been won over at
the price of a sack of ten pounds of gold. As for the two
gondoliers, they were under the impression that they were
serving the Republic. We made our start at daybreak. When
we were in the open sea, and when I remembered that night,
when I recalled all the sensations I had felt, and when I saw
again in imagination that vast treasure house, where,
according to my estimate, I was leaving thirty millions in
silver, twenty millions in gold, and many millions in
diamonds, pearls, and rubies, there came upon me something
like a fit of madness – I had the gold fever.

'We arranged to be put ashore at Smyrna, and there we at
once embarked for France. When we were getting on board of
the French ship Heaven did me the favour of ridding me of my
accomplice. At the moment I did not realise the full result of
this ill-natured stroke of chance, at which I rejoiced
exceedingly. We were so utterly unnerved, that we had
remained in a half-dazed condition without saying a word to
each other, waiting till we were in safety to enjoy ourselves as
we wished. It is not surprising that this rogue had his head a
bit turned. You will see later on how God punished me!

'I did not feel I was safe till I had sold two-thirds of my
diamonds in London and Amsterdam, and exchanged my
gold dust for notes that could be cashed. For five years I hid
myself in Madrid. Then, in 1770, I came to Paris under a
Spanish name, and had a most brilliant career there. Bianca

had died. But in the midst of my enjoyments, and when I had a fortune of six million francs at my command, I was struck with blindness. I have no doubt that this infirmity was the result of my stay in the dungeon, and of my toils when I burrowed through the stone, though perhaps my mania for seeing gold implied an abuse of the power of sight that predestined me to the loss of my eyes.

'At this time I was in love with a woman to whom I intended to unite my lot. I had told her the secret of my name. She belonged to a powerful family, and I hoped for everything from the favour shown me by Louis XV. I had put my trust in this woman, who was the friend of Madame du Barry. She advised me to consult a famous oculist in London. But after we had stayed some months in that city, the woman gave me the slip one day in Hyde Park, after having robbed me of all my fortune, and left me without any resource. For being obliged to conceal my real name, which would hand me over to the vengeance of Venice, I could not appeal to any one for help. I was afraid of Venice.

'My infirmity was taken advantage of by spies with whom this woman had surrounded me. I spare you the story of adventures worthy of Gil Blas. Then came your Revolution. I was forced to become an inmate of the Quinze-Vingts Hospice, where this creature arranged for my admission, after having kept me for two years at the Bicêtre Asylum as a lunatic. I have never been able to kill her, for I could not see to do it, and I was too poor to hire another hand. If before I lost Benedetto Capri, my jailer, I had questioned him as to the position of my dungeon, I might have ascertained exactly where the treasure lay, and returned to Venice when the Republic was annihilated by Napoleon. . . .

'However, notwithstanding my blindness, let us go back to Venice! I will rediscover the door of the prison, I shall see the gold through its walls, I shall smell it even under waters beneath which it is buried. For the events that overthrew the power of Venice were of such a kind that the secret of this treasure must have died with Vendramino, the brother of Bianca, a Doge who I hoped would have made my peace with the Council of Ten. I wrote letters to the First Consul, I proposed an arrangement with the Emperor of Austria, but every one turned me away as a madman! Come, let us start for Venice, let us start even if we have to beg our way! We shall come back millionaires. We will repurchase my property and you shall be my heir. You will be Prince of Varese!'

In my astonishment of these revelations, which in my imagination assumed all the aspect of a poem, and looking at this grey head, and the dark waters of the ditches of the Bastille, stagnant water like that of the Venetian canals, I made no reply. Facino Cane concluded doubtless that I judged him as all the rest had done with a scornful pity, and he made a gesture that expressed all the philosophy of despair.

The narration had perhaps carried him back to his days of happiness at Venice. He seized his clarionet and played in a melancholy tone a Venetian air, a barcarolle, and, as he played, he regained the skill of his first years, the talent of a patrician lover. It was something like the lament by the rivers of Babylon. But gold soon reasserted its mastery.

'That treasure!' he said to me, 'I always see it, as in a waking dream. I walk about in the midst of it. The diamonds sparkle, and I am not as blind as you think. The gold and the diamonds illuminate my darkness, the night of the last Facino Cane, for my title goes to the Memmi. Mon Dieu! the murderer's punishment has begun soon enough! Ave Maria. . . .'

He recited some prayers which I could not hear.

'We shall go to Venice!' I said to him, when he rose.

'I have found a man, then!' he exclaimed, and his face lighted up.

I gave him my arm and took him home. At the door of the Quinze-Vingts he grasped my hand, while some of the guests from the wedding party passed on their way home with deafening shouts.

'Shall we start tomorrow?' said the old man.

'As soon as we have a little money.'

'But we can go on foot. I will beg alms. I am strong, and one feels young when one sees gold in front of one.'

Facino Cane died that winter after two months of lingering illness. The poor fellow had a catarrh.